BENEATH THE SHADOWS

BENEATH THE SHADOWS

KELLYANNE HALE

Charleston, SC
www.PalmettoPublishing.com

First Edition

Paperback ISBN: 979-8-8229-1022-5

ACKNOWLEDGMENTS

Thank you very much to Councillor Reid of Beith, Scotland, for your expertise and taking the time to answer my questions, share your stories, and encourage me in this journey.

Thank you to my dearest friend, Sue. I appreciated your honesty and assistance throughout this process.

Thank you, Dale, for sharing insights on Scottish culture. The day you told me you were proud of me gave me such an adrenaline rush to finish this book.

Thanks, Greg, for always asking, "How's the 'clootie' book coming?" The jokes and ideas always helped me press on!

Thank you, Emma Restall Orr and Philip Shallcrass of the British Druid Order from the Isles of Britain. I hope in some way I properly represented the Druid culture spiritually and respectfully. May blessings always fill your grove.

Chapter 1

FOR SCOTLAND!

The fall air lay over the town of Beith like a light morning dew. As the sun broke through the clouds, the rays brought their radiance to the dreary town. Yet the birch trees hadn't surrendered the colorful leaves of reds and oranges quite yet. The slight breeze made small ripples in the lochs nearby, and the rays glistened upon them like tiny diamonds.

Mornings like these gave the townspeople hope even after fifty years of oppression. It was the age of the boy king—King Archibald VII. He had been only eleven years old when crowned king of England after two planes crashed carrying precious cargo—the royal family. The king of Cambridge, King Louis, and queen consort, Queen Gretchen—King Archibald's aunt and uncle—and his cousins, Princess Beatrice, Prince Andrew, and Prince Albert, all died due to a microburst or some weather anomaly over the Atlantic. King

Archibald was furious at the idea of becoming anything royalty since his parents had promised him a normal life, one without so much responsibility like his cousins had. *Dress this way, act all proper*—it was all too much for the king to comprehend. The promise had been made after his parents were stripped of their titles from the king's grandmother. Only rumors shadowed the truth, and King Archibald still didn't know the full story. The only truth known at this juncture was that Archibald was king at the age of eleven.

Archibald became full of fury. The councillors to the king tried to comfort him, but it was no use. It was like a toddler's temper tantrum as he refused to listen to reason, rebelling against those who tried to help. He renounced God because he had been forced to be something he felt he wasn't called to be. He was supposed to be a child! Playing rugby, learning to hunt the great stag of Scotland, riding his bike through the streets of London, playing kickball—but not be a king. Archibald hadn't had a choice, and he was now king. He now had to act and be a certain way, like his cousins. No freedom. The hatred of his situation grew, and he ordered that the old ways of Druidism replace Christianity.

This law expanded into Scotland and the predominantly Catholic Ireland. Nothing like this had happened for over a millennium. Unfortunately, the boy king's temper tantrum paved the way to the current beliefs and misfortunes in Beith, Scotland.

Dawn Erskine, a well-educated woman who had studied at Yale and the University of Edinburgh, was elected the second minister of Scotland at the age of thirty. Her intelligence, fiery attitude, and proud demeanor were the perfect fit for fighting for an independent Scotland. Even more so now with a new boy king ruling over the whole United Kingdom. The thought of it made her shake her head with despair, but not so much as to give up. If anything, it made her feel like she could rise above the previous ministers and finally do what they couldn't. Make an independent Scotland.

Erskine was due to make her very first public speech in Glasgow. Normally, Edinburgh, the capital, would have been the likely place; however, she wanted to go where she could reach the people, not just those that were high class or were already for an independent Scotland. She needed to reach those that were middle- to lower-class citizens. Those that needed to fully understand what an independent Scotland would bring them now and for the future. She was tough as nails but also had a pure heart, one that was for Scotland! All of it! Its heritage, its history, its people—everything Scotland.

People were gathered in the local pubs, department stores, and any location with a tele. Police in riot gear were at the ready for any confrontations to arise. The correction officers at the nearby HMP Barlinnie Prison were also ready to accept new disorderly prisoners. This wouldn't be the first time a riot would break out and end up in the hands of correction officers. As people were anxiously waiting for the speech to begin, the local news reporter, Stephanie McGowen, made her announcement.

"Stephanie McGowen reporting from Glasgow Center Square. I am getting a notification right now that the second minister is just moments away from making her first inaugural speech. From what I have heard thus far, she is going to speak about an independent Scotland. Let us ask some people how they would feel about that," she stated.

The camera then moved to her left, and a slender young man appeared with short reddish hair, wearing a jumper and jeans. The caption on camera read David Robertson.

"What are your thoughts about possibly having an independent Scotland?" she asked him.

"I think it would be about time actually. We are able to sustain our businesses, accept imports and exports. However, I am worried about taxes, wages, and medical. Our taxes are too high, wages too low, and our medical wouldn't be free. Just wondering how our second minister is going to make up for all that," Mr. Robertson stated eloquently.

"Those are some excellent questions that I hope she addresses today or soon. Thank you. Oh, I'm hearing she is arriving to the podium. Let's head there now," Ms. McGowen said as the camera focused on the second minister arriving to the podium.

"Good afternoon, citizens of Scotland. I want to thank all of you for this opportunity to serve you as your second minister. We have been on this road before. Time and time again, we have failed to make that shift to an independent Scotland. Well, on this day, September twelfth, 2030, I, second minister of Scotland, declare it is time to become independent from England and a new united Scotland!"

You could hear from most all of Glasgow the cheers, which seemed to be in harmony with one other. She continued, saying, "History has proved many times, from our beloved Queen Mary to William Wallace to our Nathan Maclury, that when we become a united Scotland, we fight to the death for what we believe in. We have proved that we can live and prosper separated from English rule. We cannot stand idly by and allow this boy king to make hasty decisions that affect us all!"

Before she could continue, the crowds in the streets roared with agreement and began to chant, *Go to war! Go to war! Go to war!* Yet war was really not an option in her mind. She continued by adding, "We are a strong Scotland, just like the times of old. We must bring this fury back if we are going to stand our ground! The time has come to be an independent Scotland! Negotiations will commence next week; as I have shown you already, I will not take no for an answer!"

All of Scotland was cheering while England stewed at the idea of an independent Scotland. King Archibald was not pleased, nor those from the royal court. But soon King Archibald would have to face this woman and make some harsh decisions. Councillor Gary tried to assure His Highness that he would have nothing to worry about when meeting the second minister.

"Your Highness, Scotland has been pressing this issue for eons and has failed every time. No woman of her low status can promise such a change," he said nonchalantly.

King Archibald had a look of discernment, his eyebrows inward, and pondered the notion for a moment. In a quiet tone, he replied, "Councillor, may I remind you that although I am eleven, I'm not too naive. I have you and many others to steer me in the proper direction that will benefit all of England. Did we not have a queen, the longest-reigning one, rule England and many territories for over seventy years? Did we not have the beloved people's princess do more than any other princess for the sake of England? And my mother, stripped of her status because she, too, stood up to the late queen? Be wary the next time you speak against any woman and their 'status,' for it may be the last time you speak at all!" the king stated with a quiet and sharp tone.

Councillor Gary flushed in the face as though he were about to be beheaded at that moment, swallowed his breath, and replied, "Forgive me, Your Highness." King Archibald looked at Councillor Dwight Gary in disgust as though he were a bug and then continued speaking.

"Prime Minister, councillors, gentlemen, never underestimate a woman and her capabilities. We will give this second minister a chance to state her claims. I will deny her, and we can go about our day," the king stated with a cheeky smile.

The royal court cheered, "Hear! Hear!" followed by haughty laughter. It seemed like the perfect moment to break out the cigars and end the session for the day.

King Archibald felt like an adult. For the first time, he felt as though he was taken seriously. But at what cost? The cost of Scotland? England? And taken seriously by whom? The royal court? Citizens of England? In a week's time, King Archibald would have to face his next dilemma: the second minister.

The day came. It was like people taking their places for the first showing of a play.

The second minister and her staff arrived in Winslet Palace to discuss Scotland's independence.

As the black SUVs with limousine-esque dark-tinted windows arrived, they were greeted by royal guards in their navy-blue trousers, wide white belts, red tunics with golden shoulder and button accents, and navy-blue berets. Their stern looks never faltered as it was very serious to ensure the guards always kept eyes on the *guests* and, of course, protected the king.

The second minister and her staff were then escorted to the Hall of the Royal Court Assembly, where all official meetings took place. The two grand doors were opened by two guards, one on each side, who shut the doors simultaneously once the guests were inside the assembly area.

Where they entered stood a highly finished wooden podium facing the king's chair. About one meter forward and to the left and right of the podium were seven long benches made of the same oak wood as the podium, which sat ten in each row. The number seven was because there were three colors in England's flag and four stripes representing the Cross in the form of an X. The room was surrounded by slate pillars standing eighteen meters high, and in between each pillar were paintings of previous kings and queens of England with the majestic purple-and-gold backdrop. Above the pillars were arch-topped stained-glass windows with each next to a pillar with the royal family crest branded into each one. As the sun shone through the windows, a blue hue danced upon the pillars. Toward the ceiling was an intertwined gold kaleidoscope, which enhanced the painting of a battle, presumably from the 1600s, surrounded by angels and demons alike. It was powerful yet humbling. As it represented, in battle, we are never safe from sword or spear.

As the second minister approached the podium, her gait sent a message to all present that she had already won this battle. Her head held high, with her long copper-red hair perfectly straight in the back and the front against her black suit, she wore black three-inch heels and black sheer tights that had a damask design that showed on the sides of her legs. Her blue eyes, which seemed electric, like a neon sign, stared across the room directly at the boy king. The royal court shuffled a bit in their seats as though they felt intimidated by her. She did a slight curt-sy to the young king.

"Your Majesty," she said softly.

King Archibald responded, "I suppose you think you are my equal."

Without thinking twice about her response, the second minister responded sternly, "Yes, actually, hence why I'm here today."

"I could make you bow properly, Second Minister," King Archibald said with a bit of sarcasm.

"I'm not here for your childish games, Your Majesty. You may wear the crown, but it doesn't mean you're a suitable king!" the second minister exclaimed.

There was a gasp from almost everyone in the room. She stood firm, yet in the back of her mind, she knew if she provoked him further, he might spawn another temper tantrum, which could ruin negotiations.

"Your Majesty, I am not here to battle wits but only to have an independent Scotland," she stated bluntly. There was an eerie silence that swept the room. Eyes shifted back and forth as the royal court members wondered what was going to be said next. Prime Minister Allen Reid stood up to attempt to intervene.

"Your Majesty, if I may…"

King Archibald interrupted. "No, you *may* not."

Prime Minster Mead took a deep breath, adjusted his jacket, and sat back down as reticence blanketed the room. Erskine was getting impatient with the king's antics, and the time-wasting back-and-forth nonsense needed to stop!

"Your Majesty, allow me to be very clear as to why I'm here. I am not asking for permission but to negotiate the terms in order to regulate a smooth transition to independence," she said firmly.

"I know why you're here, Second Minister," he said arrogantly.

If a face could tell a story, Erskine spoke a novel. Words that even wee ones should never hear. Her mind was going a mile a minute, and her teeth were champing at the bit to say what she wanted to say rather what should be said. She had to remember her purpose. She couldn't disappoint her people, her country.

"Let me ask you a question, Your Majesty: Other than ancestry that was married into your current lineage, what do you hold dear about Scotland?" she asked as though she had just called *check* in a chess match. She continued. "You have relatively no ties to Scotland. You don't know its history, let alone its people. The only time you sassenachs come to Scotland is to kill some stags and have a holiday!" Erskine stated firmly yet low toned so it didn't portray actual disrespect. Not quite checkmate, but hopefully in a few more moves, this meeting would end. There were gasps and susurrations among the gentlemen.

Without Erskine outright saying it, the young king's authority was being challenged. Her seeming disrespect to the king caused the royal court to think what was guaranteed for brandy and cigars had just gotten derailed to uncertainty.

"Silence!" King Archibald yelled.

The prime minister covered his mouth and murmured, "Oh shit."

The king locked his eyes on hers. She was known for not keeping her nonverbals at bay. You would know exactly what she was thinking without her saying a word. It was clear as she had one eyebrow raised and looked like she would say something sarcastic. She thought to herself, *What grand speech is this wee laddie going to surprise us with?*

The king got up from his seat and slowly walked toward her with his hands behind his back, head held high, and walking astutely as though he were a professor at Cambridge. Everyone stood as he walked through the middle of the royal court. The prime minister took his handkerchief to wipe his forehead as he sweat in a panic. The gentlemen next to him fanned him as though it would help in some way. The king reached the podium and said calmly, "Bow to me, Second Minister."

Looking down at him, she responded, "I will do no such thing!"

The king raised his voice and demanded again for her to bow to him.

"Where is the royal mother to whip your wee arse for this intolerable nonsense?" she asked directly.

At this point, the prime minister fainted. The gentlemen were trying to get him conscious, but their efforts were to no avail. The king and the second minister stood silent, eyes locked on each other and both filled with rage. Something needed to be said and quick, or anything that was said next would likely cause an outright war.

Councillor MacDuffie of Aberdeen walked to the center of the court and exclaimed, "Silence! I said, silence! This has become very exasperating, and we need to calm ourselves for the sake of both England and Scotland!"

"I'm sorry, who is king here?" King Archibald said sarcastically.

"Your Majesty, you are, of course. However, as part of your royal court, it is also my duty to give proper counsel," Councillor Robert MacDuffie said. He stood roughly 180 centimeters, with his lengthy build, hazel eyes, distinctive thick white eyebrows, and short white hair. His hair was thick and didn't have to be combed over. His voice was baritone and would carry as though his voice echoed over many mountains.

King Archibald appreciated his councillors, and at this particular moment, he would have to find a way to calm himself, but he still needed to be in control. Both Councillor MacDuffie and the second minister needed to respect his authority.

"You have both wisdom and knowledge, Councillor MacDuffie. Just remember who has the authority here," the king said.

"Of course, Your Majesty," Councillor MacDuffie said with a slight bow for affirmation.

"As for you, Second Minister, I invite you and your entourage for dinner this evening. Please wear proper dinner attire. Councillor MacDuffie will show you to your rooms. Please don't try to say no. I have already decided that you are staying for dinner," King Archibald said with a smile as he walked away.

Prime Minster Mead finally woke up from his dramatic fainting spell.

"Oh my! Are we going to war? Is everything OK? What did I miss?" he said frantically as though he had missed days of commentary.

Councillor MacDuffie said as he rolled his eyes a bit, "Get the prime minister back to his residence, please."

The other gentlemen walked him to his car, and he was sent to his home.

"Goodness! That is your prime minister? I only thought it was rumored he was a bit, shall I say, too delicate for a man of his stature? He seems easily unsettled," the second minister said.

"He is a perfectionist and wants everything to go as planned for England. Truly, I assure you, his heart is in the right place. With everything that has occurred with the royal family and the devastation it has caused the king, I'm afraid we are all on pins and needles searching for a proper balance in the situation," Councillor MacDuffie said with a sense of innocence and mild mannerism in his voice.

"I can understand. But I also hope that His Majesty and the royal court also understand our desire to be independent. Our livelihood could fall victim of dire imbalances from your king. We cannot risk that. I will not allow my country to suffer just because the king is troubled from losing his family and becoming something he doesn't want to be. That shouldn't be a burden that weighs upon *us*. You do understand, Councillor?" the second minister said, looking him dead in the eyes with eyebrows raised as if his response better be that he understood.

"Of course, Second Minister. However, I think this would be better expressed over dinner this evening. Here, let me show you to your rooms. This way, please," Councillor MacDuffie said calmly.

Councillor MacDuffie walked a few steps ahead to open the grand white doors with gold trim. It looked very luxurious for a guest room. As they entered the room, a queen-size canopy bed was to the left with damask cotton in navy blue with some small tassels on each corner of the pillowcases and the edges of the down-filled duvet. The bed also had two sheer curtains on each side, tied to the ends of the bedposts with golden ties and matching tassels. The room was blanketed with the scent of freesia. The light-gray-with-navy-blue Aarhus-designed rug was recently cleaned; the lines from the steam cleaner were a giveaway.

Directly in front, on each side of the wall, were two large round-topped windows that overlooked the grandiose garden with perfectly manicured, evenly spaced bushes and trees; flowers of pink and yellow; and bright-red roses. Definitely odd for this time of year, yet it was nice to see the pink potentillas still in bloom, along with the pink-and-purple fuchsias still brightening the freshly cut lawn. In the center was a three-tiered water fountain that spouted water from the top, which then evenly flowed into the basin below. The stones that filled the inside of the basin and the three tiers above it were of a slight-blue hue—the same color that resembled the color of light coming from the windows in the Royal Court Assembly. Toward the back of the main garden were patches of little islands surrounded by flowing water, which seemed to come from the large fountain. There was a walkway that led to each island, and each island had some shrubbery along with different-colored flowers. This was where the king presumably took his walks to get a little bit of distance from being a king and time to just be a boy.

Between the two windows stood a vintage vanity of finely polished oak, with two drawers side by side that had gold dropped handles. The legs were cabriole legs with S curves and a golden plate on the top part of each leg with a rose branded into it. Directly to the right was a long standing oval-shaped mirror, and its stand matched the wood and polish of the vanity.

The walk-in closet was fairly simple, with two long racks on each side. The second minister's clothes were already hung and evenly spaced, giving the indication that this was common practice or someone on the staff was a little OCD. As you came in, directly to the right was a sitting area furnished with a light-gray couch with navy-blue pillows and center in front of the couch was a round wooden coffee table. On the wall was a sixty-inch-wide-screen television; just below the television was a brass two-tier cart with an enticing minibar with some Macallan whisky, red and white wine imported from Italy, and other full bottles of alcohol that could knock out a horse for two days. Nevertheless, it was a welcoming luxurious room.

Next to the bed was a door that led to the grand washroom. As you entered, on the right was a place to hang robes, and to the left was a small shelving unit filled with towels. Farther to the left was a double sink with golden taps. Adjacent to the sinks was the bidet. At the very back was a stand-alone large Jacuzzi bath, and in the corner was a shower. Pillar candles on floor candelabras stood on each side of the Jacuzzi, and fresh flowers—roses, freesias, and lilies—decorated the room.

Erskine went back to sit on the edge of the bed. She remembered that at times when life was tough to manage, her beloved, Bruce, would comfort her. She grinned. He was a gorgeous man with white hair cut short with a slight swoosh at the top. His eyes were a crystal blue, and when you looked deeply into them, it was like looking through a kaleidoscope. He was slender yet muscular, and his arms made her feel safe. His lips, thin yet warm, and his kisses, powerful yet sweet, would make you forget about anything. He had an odd sense of humor that not many would understand, but anytime she was a bit distressed, he would say things like, *Oh, for fuck's sake, woman, quit your greetin'. You'll be fine.* It sounded harsh, but he would hold her and then smile with his snarky grin. She needed him more than ever now.

Tears started flowing from her eyes. Two years ago to the day, she had been told her love was killed in a riot, which devastated her to her core. He was a sergeant and team lead on Edinburgh's police force and was always first to enter danger. This particular riot had become extremely hostile, and he got stabbed in the back of the neck. The person who was supposed to have his back also got killed. Needless to say, the killer received life in prison, was sent to HMP Barlinnie, and was properly shown the staircase and other rooms during his detainment. Since then, Erskine had no desire to find another love. Her heart was always where he was, and he was no more.

After a good hour's rest, she rose from bed just long enough before there was a knock at the door.

"Enter," the second minister said. She presumed it was her lady's maid to prepare her for the grand supper. She presumed correctly.

"My lady," Freya said as she made a quick curtsy. "My name is Freya, and I will be assisting you this evening," she added.

"Hello, Freya. How has your day been thus far?" the second minister asked.

Freya looked very confused as no royal, royal guard, or anyone else for that matter ever asked her how her day was.

"Ah, my lady, it has been busy as usual. My main jobs were to see the grand room was properly ready for guests and to assist you, my lady," Freya responded.

"Well, I'm certain the grand room looks absolutely splendid. And of course I am appreciative for your service. I normally do everything myself, but when in Rome, I guess," the second minister stated with a gentle smile. Although her words were sincere, there was a hidden agenda: to get intel. You got it with honey, not vinegar.

"My lady, just so you know, and I must pride myself a bit, I'm the best with hair and makeup," Freya stated proudly.

"Well, you won't have to worry about the makeup, but hair? Make it your perfection!" Erskine said.

Freya smiled and brought out the flat iron, curling iron, and pins to get started on the hair. About fifteen minutes in, Freya started looking nervous. Breathing heavily, biting her lip, shifting her eyes as if she couldn't concentrate.

"Is everything all right, lassie?" Erskine asked with legitimate concern.

"My lady, if I may be bold?" Freya asked nervously.

"Of course, lassie! Before you faint—please!" Erskine exclaimed.

"My lady, many of the help have been chatting about a possible war. I have my mum in Lanark, and—" Freya started to say, then the second minister cut her off abruptly.

The second minister turned around in her chair and looked directly at Freya's face and said, "It is not my intention to have a war; however, it is time to be our own country and not be pinned down by a lineage that is centuries old and proved not to be beneficial. Yes, free college and medical is nice, yet it comes with a price from taxes and reforms, and due to the imbalance, proper wages suffer as well. I want to bring back balance to Scotland, but we must be independent to do so."

"Thank you, my lady. Please allow me to freshen up a bit," Freya said with a sigh of relief.

"Of course! No need to be nervous, lassie. We are nearly finished anyway," the second minister said calmly.

Freya went to the loo and washed her hands. She then took out the mini digital recorder from her pocket and turned it off. The king wanted her to get as much information as she could, but Freya realised the second minister meant no harm to her people or those in England. She placed the recorder back in her pocket and had to figure out what to say to the king later on. Freya opened the door and walked briskly back to tend to the second minister.

"You OK now?" the second minister said with a slight smile.

"Very much so, my lady," Freya responded with a smile as she started curling parts of the second minister's hair.

"Good. We wouldn't want the king to think I made you upset," the second minister said with a smirk. Freya's eyes widened, but she didn't look to see if the second minister was looking at her. Then she responded. "Of course, my lady. OK, now time for the dress!" Freya said as she walked toward the closet. "Which dress did you have in mind, my lady?" she asked.

"The dark-blue one should be appropriate," the second minister said.

"Very well, my lady," Freya said. She took the dress off the hanger. The second minister stood in her navy-blue lace bra and matching lace panties, which hooked to her thigh-high stockings to keep them in place. She stepped into the navy-blue sequined dress, Freya zipped up the back, and then the second minister picked up her shoes. She delicately slipped a foot into her three-inch-heeled shoe as though a prince was putting on her glass slipper. Then she slipped on the other one just as gently. Freya did her checks upon the second minister to look for wrinkles, hair misplacement, and anything else that would make her less than perfect. She was ready to address the king.

Chapter 2

THE INTERNAL WAR

Right at 6:15 p.m., one of butlers entered the room and announced dinner was served. Everyone stood up and allowed the king to walk out the door first, followed by the president of Ireland, second minister of Wales, and random dukes and earls that were once twelfth through twentieth to the throne but had moved up the line since King Archibald was crowned. The king suddenly stopped midway through the foyer and looked up at the grand domelike ceiling, mesmerized by the art, and addressed his audience.

"If memory serves me correctly, the angels and demons are in the midst of war." He gazed at Second Minister Erskine and continued, "There is some irony to it, as though the picture displayed was meant for a different era. Do you agree, Second Minister?" And before she could even answer, King Archibald and the other royalty moved closer to the dining room. She was infuriated that the boy king seemed to have made up his mind. She wanted to slap the cheeky grin off his face but had to keep reminding herself that she was there for one purpose, and that was to seek independence for Scotland.

As they walked into the grand dining room, the wait-staff was stationed three feet from each corner of the table, dressed in their absolute best attire. Each setting was earthenware from the early 1800s with blue accents on the edges and what appeared to be large thistles garnishing the center. There were folded notecards indicating the seating arrangement. The second minister sat adjacent to the boy king, clearly so he could keep an eye on her and her facial expressions. She knew that the king would try to antagonize her every chance he could just to get a proper rise out of her. She knew that he would also try to embarrass her in front of the other royalty to show her that the loyalty around the table lay with him. She knew no one wanted a war, whether they were loyal to the boy king or not. Yet if no independence terms could be made, would the others potentially support England in a war on Scotland?

"I hope you don't mind, Second Minister Erskine. I took the liberty of having our staff cook a proper Scottish meal since of course you are the reason why we are all here," King Archibald stated. The staff was busy trying to fluff up his pillow in the adult-sized chair.

"That was very thoughtful, thank you," the second minister retorted, giving a slight nod of gratitude. Then she followed up with a dim rhetorical question. "Yes, why are all the other gentlemen here?"

"Well, as you know, Second Minister—and I do believe that I can speak for many of us here—we do not welcome a war," President O'Hare stated.

"That is not what Scotland wants at all! We just need our independence. It is what the people want," Erskine said.

"If it does come to a war, Northern Ireland does not want to fight but will support the king!" President O'Hare stated profoundly. "Nobody wants a war. We have enough troubles in our own country—you know, Sinn Féin, the IRA, and unfortunately, a few more that we are discovering. War would send my country into an uproar."

"Yet, with all your *troubles*, as you so stated, President O'Hare, you are still able to support the war. Would that not put your country in more of an uproar with those that don't support England? Tell us, then, what threats have the king and his counsel expelled upon you to keep you in the potential fight?" Second Minister Erskine asked. She then took a spoonful of the red-lentil-and-barley soup. "Oh my. The soup is quite delicious! Well done!" she added.

"You have to understand, Second Minister, our hands are tied here," President O'Hare stated.

"I think it is clear where we are in this," Second Minister Hughes stated. Wales was a small country attached to the hip of England and certainly couldn't risk being detached. When England moved, they moved, like a waltz. An intimate dance where two move with grace. Yet the second minister couldn't help but notice the look in Second Minister Hughes's eyes that showed deep concern, as though he knew what was to come.

"Ah yes! The main course! Haggis! Second Minister Erskine, please do take the first bite and tell us how it fares compared to how it's made in your home," King Archibald said as he readjusted in his makeshift high chair.

"It would be my pleasure," she said with a slight smile.

"Second Minister, allow me to take the first bite. It could be poisoned," Agent Heisenberg said. Agent Wilson went to grab her bowl and replace it with his, but she stopped him and looked at both Heisenberg and Wilson with appreciation.

Agent Keith Heisenberg came from a small town in England called Marton. He moved to Scotland in his early thirties and received his master's degrees in criminal justice and global security from the University of Glasgow. After the first minister was murdered, there had been a call for increased security in Edinburgh. Agent Heisenberg was top of his class, met every qualification, and was chosen by the second minister to serve as part of her security team.

Agent David Wilson, a.k.a. Battle Swine, received his nickname at the University of Edinburgh after completing his martial arts training. The professor challenged people in the class to capture a pig, which apparently was a running joke between the arts and geosciences departments. Agent Wilson was the only one that caught the pig, hence his nickname. He came from East Kilshire, and fighting was in his nature; however, he wanted something different, so he, too, received a master's degree in global security. Two things were certain with both agents: they were loyal to the second minister and loyal to Scotland.

"No need for concern, young man," King Archibald said. The second minister and Heisenberg looked up at the king when he spoke. He added, "You have quite the entourage. Very loyal. Now, on with the haggis!"

The second minister looked at Agents Heisenberg and Wilson as if to tell them everything was fine.

One of the waitstaff placed a double portion of haggis on Erskine's plate along with tatties, fresh green beans wrapped loosely in bacon, cooked neeps, and fresh plain loaf bread. As the second minister looked at the beautiful display, she almost forgot that she was in a castle, elegantly dressed, and there for a purpose. She wanted to dive in like a Viking before battle.

"Sir, if you could please…," Erskine started to ask.

"I am already on it, my lady," he responded as he poured the best Scottish whisky.

The second minister raised her glass and proposed a simple but powerful toast.

"TO SCOTLAND!" she exclaimed as she and her agents slammed back the whisky.

Everyone but her agents looked at her with utter shock. The dukes looked at her like she was a heathen, and she could see President O'Hare and Second Minister Hughes each hiding a slight smirk. Yet all replied, mollifyingly, of course, "To Scotland."

Second Minister Erskine took a hearty bite of haggis. "Your Highness. You cheated," she said with a snarky grin. "It's all sheep, with oatmeal, suet, and spices. Your chef must be from Scotland."

"I must say, Second Minister, you are a true Scotsman!" King Archibald said.

"Keep the whisky coming, please," Erskine said.

"Right away, my lady," he replied as he poured the whisky.

The Duke of Grafton and the Duke of Beaufort were both in their midforties, both unwed, and to say they were quite prudish was merely an understatement.

"My, this is quite an acquired taste. You said it was all sheep; do I dare ask what part of the sheep?" the Duke of Grafton asked.

Second Minister Dawn Erskine just looked at him with a devious smile and said, "Oh, just the insides of the sheep—the heart, liver, and lungs. The suet is the fat from the sheep or other animals to give it the robust flavor." She continued to eat her neeps and beans wrapped in bacon.

After she finished her meal, the waitstaff brought out some Dundee cake, which was made with cranberries, slightly covered with an orange-zest frosting, and sprinkled with almonds. Erskine took a bite, and it tasted like heaven, like home. The cake was moist and the cranberries so juicy. The orange zest was not overpowering nor sugary. Absolutely perfect.

It was half past seven, and the moment came to discuss the future of Scotland's independence. This was going to be the moment where history would meet the path of freedom—the freedom many had fought for so many centuries ago.

There was still some idle chatter, until the king rose from his plush chair. Then everyone followed him into the royal lounge. The chaises and chairs were situated in a rectangular formation. After they walked in, the king wasted no time in beginning the meeting.

"Let us begin. This meeting will be short, and I will not be bothered by this any longer. Although you have eighty-five percent of Scotland's population wanting an independent Scotland, according to the referendum, and it's clear what Scotland would be voting for, I, however, am not willing to give up power. There will be no war as the military belongs to me. You would lose. Do I make myself abundantly clear, Second Minister?" King Archibald stated. It was clear that he'd had assistance from his royal court because he couldn't understand the referendum if he tried.

"Your Majesty, surely you and the royal court can relook at the referendum and absolutely conclude that Scotland can be independent and maintain positive relations with England. War is not what we want, never have, but we have worked diligently to earn our independence, and there is no reason why we cannae be that!" Erskine said with determination. She was so furious that when she spoke, her Scottish accent was powerful and almost enigmatic. The other leaders were standing around the king, holding their drinks of rum, whisky, or brandy. It didn't matter what would be said, Scotland had lost. Erskine had failed. Even Councillor MacDuffie wouldn't look her way.

"Only royalty could challenge the king," the Duke of Beaufort stated. His intimidating grin indicated he had just defeated her. It was evident they were unaware of her ace card. Although she would not see Scotland's independence in her time, Scotland would eventually have its freedom.

"It is settled, then. Scotland will remain under the Crown," King Archibald stated.

"Allow me to escort you to your room, ma'am," Councillor MacDuffie stated. He had just dismissed her a time before, and it was clear her time at the palace had ended. The gentlemen in the room didn't even look her way as she departed.

After the meeting, Erskine felt deflated. Agent Wilson asked to be excused, and his request was granted. Agent Heisenberg stayed with Erskine in the grand foyer at the base of the curved staircase. There was a pause, and Erskine looked at Agent Heisenberg, then asked, "I probably should also address this with Agent Wilson; however, I wanted to let you know that I appreciate all that you and Agent Wilson have done to protect me, which ultimately protects Scotland. With all the education you possess, why did you choose to serve me? I ask because right at this moment, I'm not sure what the future holds for Scotland. I trust you, Agent Heisenberg. You may speak freely."

Agent Heisenberg was not one for many words but was happy to oblige. He knew the severity of the situation. It was not as though what he would say would make Scotland any safer, but it would likely encourage Erskine to face her upcoming challenge.

"Second Minister," he said, standing proper as though he were addressing a respectable member of royalty, "before coming to Scotland, I had a family. I worked so hard to get the best education and get the best job to provide for them. When the opportunity arose to be part of your security team, at that moment, I felt like that would give me a sense of purpose. I told my wife, and she was totally against it. She would tell me that I was risking my life. She hated having to leave England, having to be farther away from her family. Our kids would have to start a new school. She thought I was being selfish. I told her I hadn't decided yet and wanted to further discuss it, yet she told me, 'It doesn't matter what you decide; the kids and I are staying in England.' I said, 'OK,' as in, 'OK, I won't take the offer.' The next day, after work, our house was empty, except for my belongings. Come to find out she had planned to move out all along. Not with anyone, but she fell out of love with me and where I was going in life. Last year, our divorce was final. So, to answer your question, I failed in one aspect but succeeded in another. I believe in you, I believe in Scotland, and I believe you can help make a difference for the people of Scotland."

Floored, Erskine stood in disbelief. Agent Heisenberg had sacrificed so much, and yet here he stood. Proper and without regret.

"My heart aches, Keith. You didn't fail. The situation failed you. Why didn't you tell me? I would have gladly found a replacement so you could rekindle your family. I feel absolutely depraved in feeling I am partially, if not fully, to blame in not giving you time to handle this. How can I make it up to you?"

Agent Heisenberg gave a slight smile and retorted, "What's done is done, and there is nothing anyone can do. You, my lady, have nothing to feel depraved about. Choices were made, and well, here I stand."

"Do you and the kids still see each other?" Erskine asked with concern.

"Oh, very much so. Although the younger two took a little bit of time, but they slowly came round. Please don't be concerned. Everything is fine," Agent Heisenberg said.

They walked up the staircase and discussed leaving early in the morning to return home. As they approached the door to each of their rooms, they turned to each other and said good night. Before Agent Heisenberg shut his door completely, Erskine said, "Keith, thank you."

"You are very welcome, my lady," Agent Heisenberg said as he gently closed the door.

Second Minister Erskine's alarm buzzed promptly at 5:00 a.m. Rubbing her eyes a bit, she realized she had forgotten to call the staff last night to inform them of her early departure. She calls for the waitstaff and Freya answers the phone.

"Freya, I am very sorry for this last-minute order, but my agents and I are about to head back to Scotland," Erskine said in a frantic voice.

"No trouble, my lady. One of your agents had already called last evening and made all the arrangements. Your light breakfast is on its way, my lady," Freya said in her bubbly voice.

"Freya, my dear, you are quite a lifesaver. I do appreciate you and the staff very much," Erskine said with a sigh of relief.

"Do you require any packing assistance, my lady?" Freya asked.

"No, thank you," Erskine said softly.

"Very well, then. Is there anything else I can assist you with, my lady?" Freya asked.

"Not at this moment, but again, I do appreciate all your assistance during our stay," Erskine said politely.

"Do have a safe journey home. It was a pleasure serving you, my lady," Freya said.

"Thank you, Freya. Take care," Erskine said as she hung up the telephone.

She couldn't help but remember what Freya told her about her mum in Lanarkshire. A war would simply destroy the economy, break friendships between allies, and cause disdain among the countries within the EU. Before she could ponder another thought, there was a knock at the door. Erskine opened the door, and there was a handmaid with a cart with another perfect display. It was really all too much just for breakfast, but there was no sense in saying anything.

"Where would you like your breakfast, my lady?" the handmaid asked.

"Over here is fine," Erskine said with a smile.

The handmaid rolled the cart to its new location, made a slight bow, and left. Erskine found that a bit peculiar but really didn't think twice about it. She proceeded to lift the large round silver lid from its base and saw a delightful display of poached eggs, a raspberry pastry, and some bacon. She was feeling satiated from the night before, so this was perfect. As she placed the lid to the side, she noticed a folded-up piece of paper sticking slightly out from under the dish. She hesitated for a brief moment, then opened the note.

My lady. Be advised that before you arrived, the king and his royal cabinet vowed to keep Scotland from being independent. His Majesty told his members to do whatever it takes to make it so. Get rid of this note once read. Not many can be trusted here.

There wasn't a name or a signature, and it looked as though it had been written in a rush. This could explain the behavior of the handmaid that delivered her breakfast. She finished her breakfast and packed her belongings. Soon there was a knock at the door.

"My lady, I'm here to take your luggage to the car," the butler said.

"Very well, thank you," Erskine said.

As Erskine and the two agents were about to step into the vehicle, Erskine noticed no one, not even the staff, was there for a proper send-off. It was a sign of disrespect, and the note clearly hadn't come from one of the dukes but as a true warning from the staff.

On the ride to the airport, Agent Heisenberg looked at Erskine. She noticed his gaze and looked back, then slightly shook her head no. He knew then something wasn't right, but she would tell him in due time.

"Agent Wilson," Erskine said.

"Yes, Second Minister. How may I be of service?" Agent Wilson asked.

She wanted to laugh, but she knew how literally and seriously Agent Wilson took his job.

"That is what I wanted to talk to you about. I wanted to personally thank you for your service and all that you continue to do to keep me safe," she said sincerely.

Agent Wilson had a shocked look on his face.

"Ah, well, I'm appreciative of that, Second Minister. If there is anything I could do better, I will do it," he replied.

"I have no doubt in my mind that you would," she responded.

"If you have any issues, personal issues, that need to be addressed, please do not hesitate to inform me," she said.

"Thank you, Second Minister. My mum is not well, and I have been worried about her. I have not been able to visit in two weeks," Agent Wilson said. He still kept his tough persona, but it was clear he needed to see her.

"Well, we will arrange something this week so you can see her," she said with a grin.

"Thank you. I'm very appreciative of that, my lady," he said.

Erskine was in her own world during the flight back to Scotland. She felt depleted, as though she had failed her country. In the moments leading up to meeting with the boy king, she had felt strong and confident that Scotland would rest in her hands. Now, leaving England with matters unresolved, it was becoming very clear that her time as second minister might be coming to an end. Yet the conversations with Heisenberg, Wilson, and Freya and the memory of her lost love were the only things allowing her to press on before the inevitable.

It was 11:00 a.m. when they reached the Ludwig House. The other twenty-seven cabinet and ministry members were waiting for her arrival.

"Second Minister, we assume that the meeting with the king did not go as planned," the deputy second minister stated. The deputy, Maxwell Stuart, was not only the next in line for second minister but came from the line of Mary, Queen of Scots, as well. He had both Bavarian and Scottish blood but no desire to be king. However, if difficult matters between Scotland and England continued to develop, he might not have a choice but to lead.

Deputy Second Minister Stuart stood 187 centimeters and had a medium build, thick salt-and-pepper hair cut short, deep-brown eyes, bushy eyebrows that were trimmed every two weeks, and a baritone voice that sounded like thunder when he spoke. He was the type of leader who was authoritative when needed but otherwise relaxed in nature. He didn't feel the need to be tense and uptight about things just because he was a chairperson.

All the members were seated in the main chamber room, waiting for Second Minister Erskine to discuss what had happened at the palace. Lord Cummings was on the edge of her seat, prepared to give any legal advice. Erskine just stood there at the podium, uncertain what she wanted to say or could say at this point.

Lord Danielle Cummings, originally from Edinburgh, had dedicated her life to understanding government legal issues since her father was councillor in Skye. Erskine respected her forthright demeanor and robust knowledge of Scottish laws and made sure Cummings was the forefront of her legal team.

"I feel as though the trip took me back to the time of the first minister. In no way do I mean this with disrespect, but this government has fought for Scotland tooth and nail and has accomplished the most compared to the previous ministers. We have given power and a proper democracy to our people. Employment is still on the rise, and wages are up and, importantly, equal. We have improved transportation. We have given a chance for those who want to attend university a means to do so. Our councillors are held accountable to the people in their sectors, and the people are being heard. It has been a very long road, but there would be no way to push for an independent Scotland if we first didn't prove we could be independent!" Erskine said. She was beyond frustrated and couldn't begin to imagine what a war would bring or how it would be pulled off in the first place.

"Lord Cummings, legally, what is our best option?" Erskine asked.

"Right now, a war would not be logical. Although our regiments have multiple brigades, we would not stand the chance against any naval fleet. Secondly, legally, from our recent polls, the country stands at eighty-five percent for an independent Scotland. That is up by thirty percent from ten years ago. Secondly, the referendum still has to be approved from the prime minister," Lord Cummings stated.

Erskine rolled her eyes and then said, "Well, I can assure you their prime minister probably doesn't remember that there's a referendum on the table. My personal take on the man was that he was not suitable for the position."

"Maybe we can revisit this and have the king come here. Have a more suitable conversation focused on the referendum rather than war," Stuart said.

"Proper idea, and as we all know, war is the last thing anyone wants. Even those from Northern Ireland and Wales stated that they were for England and would support them if war were to break out," Erskine responded.

"Second Minister, if England doesn't approve the referendum, even though we have the votes, Scotland will not become independent. As blunt as that is, Second Minister, in the meantime, we need to focus on EU and foreign policy. If we are to make allies and keep the ones we have, we need to develop an eminent and relevant policy to protect the future of Scotland. Also, the people need reassurance that we are not merely focused on independence and allowing other issues to dissolve," Lord Cummings stated.

"Maxwell, if you could please contact the prime minister. On second thought, it would probably be best if you contacted Councillor MacDuffie. He is more perspicacious. Let's try to schedule as soon as possible."

"Very well, Second Minister," Stuart said.

"Please clear my calendar for today," Erskine said.

"Right away, ma'am," the assistant responded.

Everyone started to quickly leave the room. They had their orders, and it felt like time was of the essence!

"Maxwell, before you go, I would like to discuss something with you, please," Erskine said. Maxwell and Erskine sat down on one of the long wooden seats. Her eyes shifted a bit, then focused on Maxwell. She looked as though this was going to be her last speech.

"Dawn. Are you all right?" Maxwell asked with grave concern.

"No, actually. I feel like I'm in grave danger," Erskine said softly.

"Your Druid ways are kicking in, I see. Every time you felt like this before, your intuition came true. It let you know your love died in that riot before you were told about it," Maxwell said delicately. Erskine looked at him despairingly. She had just had the same thought the day before, only to be reminded of it again. Maxwell noticed the look on her face.

"Dawn, I am so sorry. I was just acknowledging I understand when you start to feel a certain way," Maxwell said lovingly. She gave him a small smile.

"It's OK. I knew what you meant. But it is very important that I say this. If something were to happen to me in the next few weeks, I hope and pray that you become king. Everyone knows you and your background. It is the only way to stand against the boy king. Continue to make Scotland the land for so many to be proud of. Always think of the people. Promise me this, Maxwell," Erskine said passionately. Maxwell thought she was absolutely "aff her heid"; however, somehow, he believed her, and he would do anything to protect her.

"Thank you," Erskine said with a huge sigh of relief. Then she continued, "I appreciate all your help these past two years, and I just hope that nothing happens, but Scotland means so much to me that we can't let it falter."

Maxwell reassured her again. They both left the room, and he decided to walk the halls. There were some parts of him that knew exactly what the boy king felt: wanting to leave that part of him behind and be free from ruling anything. He felt too old for such responsibilities, but he would have to become king if he were to go neck and neck with the boy king. It would be the only way Scotland could gain England's respect.

Erskine went to one of the offices and talked briefly with Agent Wilson.

"Thank you for your patience, Agent Wilson," she said but was interrupted by Lord Cummings.

"Second Minister, excuse the interruption, but I took the liberty of contacting Councillor MacDuffie, and he agreed that in one weeks' time, the king will attend the referendum meeting."

"That's perfect. Thank you for letting me know. Just make sure the deputy minister knows," Erskine said.

"Of course, ma'am," Lord Cummings said.

"Now, back to you, Agent Wilson. How long will you need to visit with your mum?" Erskine said politely.

"Second Minister, I will definitely return prior to your meeting with the king," he responded.

"That is very generous of you, Agent Wilson. I appreciate that very much," Erskine said.

"Second Minister, of course," Agent Wilson said.

"Well, your leave starts now. Give my best regards to your mum, please, and I do hope you will do things that will relax you a bit," Erskine said with a smile.

"Indeed, I will, Second Minister," Agent Wilson said. As he walked out of the office, he took out his mobile and called an unknown person.

"She received the message, so everything is going as planned. It's no problem; I will be there." He ended the call, placed his mobile in his inside jacket pocket, and headed to his flat with a sinister smile.

Unknown to him, the deputy second minister was in the corner of the foyer, looking out the window, when Agent Wilson was having the conversation. *Who could he have been talking to?*

"Welcome, Your Highness. I'm glad you could be here today. I hope that we can come to an agreement finally that would benefit both countries," Erskine said delicately.

This was it. The day had come where presumably history would be made. There was a large display of pastries, cakes, sandwiches, and scones, with tea and coffee. Everything was immaculate.

"Please, at any time you wish to have a refreshment, Amber would be happy to serve you," Erskine said.

"I think we can skip all the pleasantries and get to the point here. Second Minister, I think we both were improper in our character the last time we spoke. However, it doesn't take away from the fact that although the referendum looks sensible, the vote that transpired over a year ago is now obsolete and requires a new vote. Of course, the prime minister, oddly, made that law a few days ago," King Archibald said nonchalantly.

"That's convenient. No matter. We will have another vote," Erskine said.

"Either way, time for an independent Scotland is not in the foreseeable future. Not that you would ever see it. You know what to do, Agent Wilson," King Archibald said as he started to turn away.

Just then, Agent Wilson came up behind Erskine and slit her throat. Blood gushed out everywhere, and as she took her last breath, her eyes turned black as night. Agent Heisenberg took his dagger and struck the boy king in his side. Once his blade locked into the king's flesh, he then attacked Wilson, grabbed his blade that struck Erskine, and stabbed him in the chest at least four times. By the time Agent Heisenberg was finished with Wilson, the king and his royal court were already gone. At that moment, Agent Heisenberg wanted to take his own life, yet he knew he had to hold on for the new regime. Silence covered the room like a ghostly mist. From behind the tables came Amber.

"Agent Heisenberg, is it safe now?" she asked, her voice shaking.

"Lassie, you're still here and safe? Are you OK? Are you hurt?" Agent Heisenberg asked.

"Yes, sir. I'm fine," Amber said. Just then, she saw the second minister on the ground with a pool of blood surrounding her and Agent Wilson on the floor as well. Then the doors flew open, and the deputy second minister and Lord Cummings entered the room. Agent Heisenberg explained what had happened while Amber tried to clean up the blood.

"Amber. Stop, lassie. It's OK," Lord Cummings said. Amber moved away. Agent Heisenberg and Deputy Maxwell Stuart delicately placed a sheet over the second minister.

"Are you now ready to become king?" Lord Cummings asked.

Maxwell stood in disbelief. How had he not seen this coming? Why would Agent Wilson betray the second minister? He remembered the conversation just a week before, hoping she was just paranoid. Second Minister Dawn Erskine had given her life for all of Scotland. The only way to repay that debt was to become king. Now standing astutely and eyes facing forward, he responded to Lord Cummings.

"Indeed. Indeed I am," he replied.

Chapter 3

THE PACT

An unexplainable darkness swept through the house and terrified everyone in it. Death left a permanent mark on the second minister in such a sinister way, and no one understood why.

Lord Cummings stood and noted, "We must keep this quiet until we notify the next of kin, sir."

"We can't do that, yet the last thing we need is an uprising. I will have to make a public announcement. In the meantime, call her mother in Edinburgh. Tell her that I will be making a personal visit tomorrow," Maxwell said.

"Very well, sir," Lord Cummings replied. She jotted some notes and briskly left his office.

Maxwell stood in awe remembering the accounts of the murder not even twenty-four hours prior. It was maddening seeing Wilson slit the second minister's throat and watching Heisenberg kill Wilson. Maxwell wondered if he should have said something when he briefly overheard

Wilson's peculiar conversation. He sat in his plush, freshly oiled coated leather chair and placed his hands over his face. So many thoughts engulfed his mind. What to tell her mother. How to tell the world that the second minister has died. Murdered! Frustration filled him as he wasn't quite ready to make decisions. Not for himself and not for Scotland. In order to be independent, he knew he had to become king. It would squash the rivalry between Scotland and England once and for all.

Lord Cummings said over the intercom in his office, "Sir, you will go live in five minutes."

"Thank you, Lord Cummings. Please tell me you were able to contact her family first," he replied.

"Yes, sir. They are anticipating your arrival tomorrow at ten a.m.," she stated.

"Brilliant. Thank you." He sighed knowing he will be live soon.

Just then, the automatic locks that held a news camera on the ceiling clicked, and the hydraulics and poles moved in unison placing the camera center facing Maxwell. Behind him stood two Scotland flags perfectly hung from their staves. He sat up straight when he saw the red blinking light, indicating he will soon go live. He crossed his hands and waited for his ten-second countdown to begin. The light turned green, indicating he was live.

"Citizens of Scotland, it is with immense sorrow to announce that less than twenty-four hours ago our beloved second minister, Dawn Erskine, passed away. We do not have all the details; however, her death is currently under investigation to rule out any foul play. During her short tenure as Second Minister, she fought with vim and vigor to make Scotland what it is today and pressed to make Scotland independent, and we will continue to work with England to make it a reality. Even with this day of great sorrow, our government must continue on without interruption. I, Maxwell Stuart, will take over as king of Scotland. As many of you know, I am a direct descendant to our great majesty, Queen Mary the first, and now will take up the crown to lead our county, not only into independence, but with your help, lead into a stronger and better Scotland. For now, our country is in a time of mourning. Please take these next two days to remember the woman who devoted her life to Scotland and its people."

The camera lights turned off and moved back into its position in the ceiling. Maxwell turned on the big-screen television, and to no surprise, Stephanie McGowen was already in downtown Glasgow. Many of the people she interviewed felt much sorrow losing the second minister. One person stated, "The second minister gave hope to many young people. Not many can say they have accomplished what she has in a such short time." Others were also happy that Scotland would soon reach independence and grateful that Maxwell decided to become king. There were mixed emotions throughout Scotland, but one emotion held true: Second Minister Dawn Erskine would be missed but never forgotten for her efforts to better Scotland. Maxwell's eyes welled with tears, which flowed like slow rivers along the Bayou.

The next morning, Maxwell and Heisenberg headed along the winding roads to Edinburgh to meet with Erskine's mum. Grey clouds filled the sky along with a cool breeze in the air reminding them that winter was near.

Meanwhile, bustling around the house were Erskine's mother, Catherine, and Catherine's sister, Deborah, and Erskine's sister, Denise, making last-minute preparations before the king's arrival.

Denise was a year older than Dawn. She had long copper wavy hair, thick brown eyebrows, green eyes, and had a slender build. She also had two beautiful daughters, Agnes and Irene, ages five and seven.

Catherine had just turned fifty-three years old a month prior but didn't look a day over forty. She dyed her hair copper to match her daughters and primarily to hide the gray. She, too, had green eyes and was not quite slender anymore, but at her age, she could be any size she wanted to be. Catherine was a no-holds-barred, to-the-point type of woman. Plus, nothing got past her. If someone thought she didn't know, they were mistaken. Her Druid ways kept her in tune with the spirits and helped her keep her family safe.

Deborah was the older sister by three years and the polar opposite of Catherine. Her personality was laconic compared to her sister, and anything that dealt with drama, she didn't want any part of it. She had brown hair, hazel eyes, and probably needed to eat more than she did. It was difficult to shop for her since she wore a size two when normally the smallest size in the store was a four.

She loved her nieces more than anything and would spoil them constantly. Of course Catherine would know when she did.

Denise was feeling anxious and wanted confirmation from her mother that her daughter would be safe. "Promise me, Mother, that you won't tell His Highness about what Agnes has done. She didn't know any better."

"Sweetheart, there is nothing to worry about, and no danger will be brought to her. Everything will be fine. I will tell the 'truth' but leave some information out," Catherine said.

"Thank you, Mum," Denise expressed with a sigh of relief.

"What do we call him?" Deborah asked.

Catherine pondered that a moment. "That's a very good question. I guess he'll tell us when he gets here. He may be the new Second Minister until he's crowned."

"Ah, good point, Mother. I just think it's nice he's coming here personally to share his condolences," Denise stated.

Deborah felt it was odd Maxwell Stuart was coming here. "Why would he come here and not have us come to Glasgow?"

Catherine gave a cunning look and said, "It's because he knew Dawn was a Druid and thinks there's a backstory."

Deborah widened her eyes and gritted her teeth, saying, "Well, you're right about that."

Their house was the first on the left mirroring the other four houses along a dead-end street. Two-story with a defined gable roof and the house painted a light yellow. A wide bay window, decorated from the inside with bronze and orange pillows, gave comfort to their Scottish Fold breed cat, Ollie. Their well-manicured dark-green lawn was a beautiful foundation to display the adorned walkway with trimmed sage and box shrub bushes and sunset orange begonias. On the inside, immediately to the left, was the grand sitting room, with a bronze-coloured couch and plush matching chairs. A large, elegant clear two-tier glass coffee table sat in the front of the couch and matching side tables next to the chairs. Random rustic-orange small vases and coasters highlighted the tables, along with an orange, tan, and brown checkered tartan-style throw folded on the back side of the couch. The scents of orange, nutmeg, and cinnamon filled every corner of the rooms, adding a warm, cozy feeling to the home.

As abrasive as Catherine could be at times, she was absolutely distraught for having to let go of Denise. "Sweetheart, this is for your safety and the lassies' safety. We cannot undo what has been done. However, everything is set up for you in Beith. It's a quiet little town, and you should be safe there. Just make sure as Agnes gets older, she doesn't conduct any callings of dark spirits, or many lives will be in grave danger." Catherine and Denise held each other for a long time. Catherine didn't want to let her go but knew the book had to be far away and hidden as much as possible. Denise and the girls headed out, and everyone hugged each other for the last time. Last for a while anyway.

Deborah and Catherine waved to Denise and the girls as they left the driveway. Deborah put her arm around Catherine, and Catherine put her head on Deborah's shoulder.

"They will be OK," Deborah said while rubbing Catherine's back. Catherine gave her a slight smile and said, "I hope you're right."

Deborah looked out the window and noticed a shiny black SUV pull up in the short driveway. "That must be them."

Heisenberg opened the car door for Maxwell. As Maxwell stepped out, he adjusted his jacket and headed to the front door. As they approached, Catherine was already prepared to address them.

"Good morning, Your Highness," Catherine said. She opened the door and indicated for them to come in.

"Oh please, ma'am, no formalities. Call me Maxwell," he said as he shook Catherine's hand.

"Well, please call me Catherine. This is my sister, Deborah," Catherine said as they all shook each other's hands.

"This is Agent Heisenberg. He was Dawn's personal guard before becoming mine. We have some questions that maybe you can answer for us," Maxwell said. The look in his eyes was mere desperation. He wanted to find the root cause of Dawn's murder.

"Please come have a seat. Would each of you like some tea?" Catherine asked. Both of them wanted tea. Catherine brought out some tea and cookies on porcelain plates with thistle designs.

While looking around the room, Maxwell stated, "This is a lovely home. Seems as though you and the neighbours also try to outdo yourselves on the landscaping. It's quite lovely."

Catherine went to sit down in one of the chairs and said, "Well, we can tell it's winter. My begonias are unfortunately withering away. But you didn't come here to talk about my yard, did ye?"

Maxwell's face turned gloomy. He placed his tea on the table and folded his hands, then said, "No."

"What questions did you have?" Catherine asked.

Maxwell looked at Heisenberg and nodded to him, directing him to ask his question. "Ms. Catherine, when the second minister died, her eyes turned pure black. Black as night with no moon illuminating the sky. I know she didn't have any health conditions, so how was this so?"

"Get comfortable, gentlemen. I believe what I'm about to tell you will answer all your questions. However, Mr. Heisenberg, the short version is that Dawn was a dark Druid. Just like a narcissist can hide their feelings and manipulate yours, she danced with the devil to become second minister." She said it so direct and nonchalant that her facial expression didn't change. Heisenberg sat up straight and became angry.

"No way, ma'am!"

Maxwell motioned to Heisenberg to calm down, but Catherine intervened.

"It's OK, Maxwell, I know it's difficult to hear."

"Forgive me, ma'am. It's just that I worked for her for years, and I didn't see anything sinister," Heisenberg said. He kept his composure but shook his head in disbelief.

"It's OK, love," Catherine said. She saw how dedicated Heisenberg was to her daughter and showed him a look of empathy. She started telling the history,

"Dawn has always been sweet and kind," Catherine started.

"Yes, always sweet," Deborah agreed.

"Our whole family has been following Druidism for years, and Dawn started following Druidism at the age of eight. In our grove, she became a bard because she loved to sing and play the bagpipes. First time she heard bagpipes, she had to learn. Oh, the notes that came out of that blasted thing when she was nine compared to when she turned thirteen went from nails on a chalkboard to pure glorious music. She tried the pan flute but didn't like it at all. We were very proud of her in her dedication to the grove. When we say that, it means she was dedicated to the spirits, the people within the grove, and making things harmonious. She would go to the bookstore all the time. That place was like a second home to her. Dawn would always get books on politics, Druidism, and science; so, we never questioned what books she brought into the house because she would eventually tell us. She graduated at sixteen from secondary school and headed to Yale for two years, then came back and started at the University of Edinburgh. That's when things started to be different." Catherine paused and looked at Deborah.

"Right, would you like more tea?" Deborah asked.

"That would be nice," Maxwell replied.

"Please, continue," Heisenberg said. Catherine was hesitant but knew they had to know the truth.

"Dawn would talk about things at school like being on the debate team or head of the online school newspaper, which is wonderful, but the way she would talk about it was anomalous. She would imply that she had to do better, be at the top of everything. We tried to reassure her that no one is perfect and just do the best you can and that we thought she was doing brilliantly. It wasn't enough for her. So, I decided to go to the school and see for myself what was really the issue. I was relieved that she felt happy to see me. Her room was nice and had two bookshelves of books. No surprise there. However, when I looked closely, I noticed a large hardcover black book with the tree of life and a serpent raised on the cover. I asked her where she got that, and she said another Druid that deals with dark magic. I told her for the safety of our grove and your friends here, it would be best if I took the book. Dawn reluctantly agreed but understood. I thought if the book was removed that things would improve, but it only got worse. When she graduated in 2025, it seemed that success was coming too easily for her. Her demeanor during campaigns seemed cutthroat, and the way she talked about others was demoralizing. Come to find out she made a blood pact with the demon she conjured from the book and that is how she had so much success. The only thing the demon asked in return was to worship him."

All of them sat in silence. Heisenberg's eyes were red, but he held back the tears. All the time he worked for her and all the times she seemed to care were all a lie.

"Where is the book now?" Maxwell asked.

"This next part, I assure you, will put fire in your blood," Catherine stated.

"There's worse?" Heisenberg asked.

"Unfortunately, yes," Catherine said. She situated herself in the chair. Her eyes were filled with despair as though life itself was drained from her. Catherine looked at Maxwell, then Heisenberg, and gave a long sigh.

"Just after Agnes turned five back in February, Dawn told Agnes about the dark book and how it could one day make her a high priestess of a grove. Agnes loved her auntie so much that she would hang on every word, even if it sounded wrong. So, in the book, in order to gain certain favours or powers, you would have to do something in return. A quid pro quo if you will. Dawn felt as though she didn't need to do her part of the pact anymore, so she just stopped. She thought if she transferred her part of the pact to Agnes, she would be released from the demon's grip. Dawn had Agnes sign her name in blood to vow to worship the demon in order to one day make her a high priestess."

"Where is the book now?" Maxwell asked.

"It's not here," Catherine quickly retorted.

"But you know where it is," Heisenberg said.

"I will say this, gentlemen, the book, along with my granddaughters, are safe. As long as they are away, and not chant from the book, they will remain safe." She paused, then slouched over a little, here fingers intertwined, and looked straight at Maxwell. "I know my daughter was murdered. It was her punishment for not keeping her part of the bargain with the demon. Only the demon can release you. When dealing with dark magic, demons are not in control of anything, but something more menacing is controlling them and using the demon as a conduit. A middleman. When you are a Druid, you cannot call upon the spirit of the hawk, and salmon and so on, and also be part of something malevolent. You have to be one or the other. Dawn tried to be both, and well, you know the result."

"Where is Agnes now? Will she be OK?" Maxwell asked. He didn't know what to think of the story but knew that Dawn was a Druid and had much intuition, especially when something dreadful was about to happen. It explained how she knew about her beloved before anyone officially told her what had happened to him.

"Like I said earlier, they are away from Edinburgh and safe. Demons don't care about your age. If you make a pact with them, it is best you keep your promise. I thought something was wrong when Dawn insisted watching Agnes as Deborah and I took Irene, my other granddaughter, shopping. Denise was at work that day. Irene had no interest in Druidism, and we respected that. When we got home, as soon as we walked in, there was a heavy, dark aura that filled our house. The next day, Dawn had left for Glasgow to work on her campaign for second minister. When she left, we never heard from her again," Catherine said. She became quiet and stared off into the distance. The reminder of what her daughter did tainted her spirit. Her eyes started to water because now she was without both daughters and grandchildren near her. No more days at the beach or the park. Family dinners or last-minute luncheons. Making crafts on rainy days or watching Disney and devouring popcorn for movie nights. It was gone. All gone!

Maxwell saw her pain, stood up, and approached her. He extended his arms and hugged her tightly. Both of them had silent tears flowing due to grieving from much loss. Not a dry eye in the room. As tough as Heisenberg was, even he couldn't hold back the tears. He felt betrayed. Never in a million years did he think that the second minister was capable of such destruction. Such evil. It was all a lie just so she could keep her second minister status.

"With your permission, sir, I would like to get some fresh air," Heisenberg said.

"Yes, of course," Maxwell replied.

Maxwell gently held each of Catherine's hands. "I am so very sorry that all this occurred the way it did. I wish I would have known earlier or done something or knew something."

Catherine gave him a wee smile and said, "There is nothing anyone could have done, but I appreciate you very much. For coming all the way out here and hearing the truth."

"My pleasure, Catherine. If you ever need to talk, please do not hesitate to contact me directly. I know people may or may not understand Druidism, but it can be lovely when people understand the beauty of it," Maxwell stated.

"That was lovely, thank you so much. I appreciate that," Catherine said. She had wiped away some of her tears and gave a genuine smile.

"I have to be on my way, but please remember to call me if you need anything. Ms. Deborah, it was a pleasure meeting you. I'm sure Heisenberg appreciates your hospitality but—"

Maxwell was interrupted by Deborah. "It is understandable, and it was a pleasure and honour having you both here."

The ride back to Glasgow was uncomfortably silent. Maxwell wasn't upset with Heisenberg as he needed time to digest what he had heard. Maxwell needed time as well, but soon, coronation plans would be underway. He would eventually have to tell people the truth about Dawn's murder.

On March 1, 2031, Maxwell Stuart became King Andrew I. He used Andrew in remembrance of his great-grandfather. Everyone throughout Scotland long waited for his first public announcement. Crowds of people stood near one of many large announcement screens hanging from some of the wide buildings. People also occupied the pubs with a pint in hand, anticipating the king's speech. A few moments later, a public service announcement aired on all screens.

"This program has been interrupted for a very important announcement by His Majesty, King Andrew the first."

"Citizens of Scotland, there are three very important matters that need to be addressed. First, it was ruled that Second Minister Dawn Erskine was murdered by

Agent Wilson. Agent Wilson was presumed to work for another unknown outside source who promised Wilson a substantial amount of funds. Because of this, we have emplaced more vetting procedures to guarantee our government's safety. I have spoken to the second minister's family and learned that from a very young age, she was very talented, focused on her studies, and determined to fight for Scotland. We shall always remember her dedication to Scotland and be grateful for her efforts. Secondly, dark Druid altars have been set up throughout Scotland, and I have placed an immediate order for their destruction. We believe, based on the second minister's murder, that dark magic was involved. In order to conduct a process of elimination to that theory, councillors within your county will see to the destruction of these altars. Lastly, I had just returned from meeting with King Archibald in London. England will soon formally announce official changes within their government; however, as for us, we are free to finally be an independent Scotland!"

Cheers roared through the cities. More pints were being poured, hugs exchanged, and people vigorously waved little Scotland flags. He continued on.

"I do appreciate all parties working together, along with our parliament, allowing in a short time window the voting for an independent Scotland and my coronation. This is what Scotland is all about. Being united. We were not meant to be ruled over but to govern our own way of life, just like our past rulers wanted it. In the next coming months, there will be changes, such as more equal wages, university tuition, and maintaining free health care. All of us working together is what keeps Scotland unified, peaceful, and more importantly, independent! We will move together into the future to maintain these attributes. Thank you."

Denise, Irene, and Agnes sat on the couch listening to the king's speech. Children were taught at a young age about politics and government because it was a way of life.

"So, what did you think, lassies?" Denise asked.

"Mummy, did Auntie Dawn get murdered because England wanted to rule us?" Agnes asked.

"That's right, love," Denise replied. It was the answer she agreed to say if the question was asked, but she knew it was because of Dawn's negotiation with demons.

Irene really wasn't into politics or wanted to learn it at this moment. "Hmm, I get it, but I really don't care. Can I go play now?" Irene asked. Denise couldn't help but give a small giggle to Irene's response. She would learn in time, she thought to herself.

"Ye, me too, Mummy. I wannae read," Agnes said. She was squirming, wanting to leave. If it wasn't a fun show to watch, then she didn't want any part of it.

"OK, but, Agnes, read only nice books," Denise said.

"OK, Mummy," Agnes replied.

Both girls went to their respective rooms. Agnes's room was decorated with a princess theme, whereas Irene's was all Christian. Crosses on her walls, picture of Jesus above her desk, and a Bible sat on her nightstand. Once Irene learned what her auntie made Agnes do, she had been scared ever since.

Agnes snooped around her mum's room a few days prior and found the dark book. Agnes just knew it was filled with weird spells and incantations that could make her a high priestess someday. It meant more to her now that her auntie is dead. She went into her walk-in closet, closed the door, and sat in the corner. Agnes had a little light, so she could see the words. Her eyes got as big as plates when the pages fanned to a new page. The book stopped on a particular page where the words were short in character, italicized, and had symbols with triangles and arrows at each of the corners. Agnes started to read out loud.

"*Um to no ti em, sum pro miss um mor tem ser vab o eti am dice re.*" When she said this, the darkness that hovered within her grandmother's house manifested within hers. Irene noticed one of the crosses started to turn upside down and shrieked a deathly scream as though demons were invading her room.

"MUMMY! HURRY!"

Denise ran to Irene's room and saw the cross was upside down. She turned and saw another do the same. She then ran into Agnes's room and didn't see her straightaway. When she opened the closet door, she was shocked by what she saw. Her little girl was reading out of the book. Denise snatched it out of her hands and yelled, "Agnes! No! Do you realise, lass, what you have done? I told you to never touch this book, and I told you why!" Denise dropped to her knees and cried. She wanted to burn the book but couldn't because of the active incantation. It could be burned only when the demon released you. The likelihood of that happening was probably never.

Denise took the book and hid it outside, far from the house, and buried it. Little did Denise know, Agnes watched her go into the field adjacent to their house. With the book buried, Agnes's behaviour became more like a typical child who loved to paint and play football. Yet darkness still loomed over the house. There were still times when the crosses would arbitrarily go upside down. Irene was just too scared to live there and eventually convinced her mum to allow her to live with her grand-mother in Edinburgh. It wouldn't be until years later that Agnes dug up the book again.

Chapter 4

BEHIND THE SHADOWS

"**H**ow many times do we have to hear that announcement? It's still a month away! We don't need a reminder of the murder that happened fifty years ago! Yet it's out of the queen's wage, so I'm not complainin'," Agnes said feistily.

"I agree! Queen Cara is so lovely. I've often wondered how she feels about circumstances surrounding the murder. She is very much for Scotland even though she's from Northern Ireland," Nancy said.

Nancy was fifty-four years old and looked more in her midthirties. She had dark-brown curly hair, long eye lashes, and unique light-brown eyes. She had been a model for most of her life and still had the hourglass figure, even after having her son. Nancy didn't miss modeling and was happy to stay at home.

"Oy, the Irish have their own issues, but glad she left all that there and didn't involve us in that treachery!" Agnes said.

"Precisely! Good queen she is, I say. By the way, is Anna all right? She looked tired but in a haze," Nancy asked with concern. She already knew the basis of her condition, but Agnes had mentioned that the thing spoke to her. Something wicked was afoot.

"Nancy, not sure how long it's been happening, but the poor lass has been this way for a week now. The scar she's had for months, but the *thing* being chatty with her is new. I talked with the school to see if I can homeschool her, but they want a doctor's note explainin' why. Like it's any of their damn business what's going on with my daughter!" Agnes said with conviction.

"What are ye goin' to do, Agnes?" Nancy asked.

"There's a doctor in Glasgow I heard understands our 'situation' here. Blimey, it's like we're cursed! The king ordered all those ridiculous temples to be torn down, yet we still endure the pain in the devil's playground. Why?" Agnes shouted out but quickly wiped her tears and got back to tidying up the kitchen.

Nancy rushed to console Agnes.

"It will be OK," she said, giving Agnes a hug. However, even Nancy had her doubts about anyone ever finding *the altar*, let alone having peace in Beith. They had been living in fear since the year 2030, with no peace in sight.

Anna took her long, hot shower, continually looking at the scar. The steam filled the air with scents of lavender and vanilla. The scar was a constant reminder of the dreadful night she lost her father. She remembered just finishing tea. Her mum had always made a huge feast as though every night was Robbie Burns night. Tender roast beef, tatties, beans, neeps, and honey bread that just melted in your mouth. They would have a wee bit of whisky but clearly not enough to have them too slouched in their chairs. Anna smiled. After dinner, they would sit around the tele watching old films. Dad had wanted to watch all the *Star Wars* sagas in order. They knew he would want to binge-watch. Daniel had been, of course, on the monitor with Laurie. He was layin' the love on thick, and it was too sickening to listen to. Sabrina had been constantly begging, or more like bargaining, with Mum to get extra sweets. Mum was a tough woman, and if she said no about something, you'd best shut up about it. Anna heard rustlings outside their living room window. She had looked around to see if anyone had noticed it.

"Did anyone else hear that?" Anna remembered asking.

"Heard what?" Dad asked with a raised eyebrow. "Nay, just the wind, lass. You ready for the films?" he asked with excitement, clearly ignoring Anna's concern.

"Sure, Dad," she had said with a look of uncertainty. She looked out the window. It was dark, and the only light was from the porch light, and the branches on the old birch tree weren't moving. She figured if she were to briefly look outside but didn't go down the driveway, she would be OK. She slowly crept her way to the front door, turned both bolt locks until a loud click sounded, and opened the door.

Just then, her dad noticed her in the doorway and yelled, "ANNA—NO!" He jumped up from the couch to get to her, and when he had her arm, the shadowed figure appeared and said, "You will be her sacrifice."

Mum, Sabrina, and Daniel came running, but by then, Dad was gone. She had stood in the doorway in shock, door still wide open. Mum slammed the door shut and screamed, "No! No! My Thomas! No!"

Daniel had tried to console Mum, but she wouldn't stop greetin'.

"What did you see?" And just when Sabrina had asked the question, she then immediately exclaimed, "Anna! Your arm!" It was as though Anna had been cut but healed by fire at the same time.

"What did it look like?" Sabrina asked. When she asked, you could hear a pin drop, it was so quiet. All eyes were fixated on Anna.

"I'm not quite sure. It was as though the dark figure was a shadow but made of clouded mists. When it took Dad, for a split second, it almost looked human in the face. It expanded its ghostly wings, covered Dad's mouth, flew up, then dove into the ground and vanished. It happened so fast I'm not sure of anythin' else. Please forgive me, Mum! I'm so sorry!" Anna remembers saying while greetin'. Mum was still greetin' as well. Crying, feeling devastated, all Anna had wanted was instant forgiveness. She felt like she'd just murdered her father. How could she have let that happen?

Mum then said to her, "We must keep that door closed at night, no matter what! It was bound to happen, Thomas having his fits over the loss of his brother the month before. Come along, we must tell the MPs what happened so they can mark it on their books," Mum had said angrily but then finished calmly.

Anna still didn't feel as though she'd gotten the forgiveness she was looking for. However, it was all she thought about when she saw the scar. It still looked the same as it had four months before. Only it glowed red during certain times. Times when it was still a mystery.

Anna stared out the window, noticing the sway of the trees from the breeze and the leaves flickering from the sun. The only solace she had was going to the quarry to pick up gems. Since the incident, Anna had become quite the jewel crafter.

When she entered her room, the bed sat immediately to the right, a large walk-in closet to the left. In front of the bed was a double-pane window with a wide ledge, looking out over the cul-de-sac to the other four two-story houses. Then along the wall were two elongated workbenches that Thomas had made for her, filled with jewel-crafting items, such as files, pliers, a small butane torch, soldering equipment, old rings without settings, polishing brushes, and of course crystals from Loanhead Quarry. Only the newest and best equipment was required because one slipup could cause the gem or crystal to lose its value.

After the floods of 2060 throughout the United Kingdom, there were rumours of gems surfacing along lochs and streams. Anna didn't hesitate to adventure to the nearby quarry and find these rumours to be true. She was fascinated by the colour clarity of lava oranges and the bloodred gems that reminded her of the Arizona sunsets she had read about in a recent book and deep-blue gems that matched the colour of her eyes. Finding gems and making jewelry for her mum gave her confidence and allowed her not to feel so guilty about her father. This day was no different. She tied her long wavy golden hair into a messy bun, grabbed her wellies, and backpack of needed supplies, and headed down the stairs.

"I'm off to the quarry, Mum," Anna said with a little excitement.

"You sure you're up to it, love?" her mum asked with uncertainty.

"Yes, better now," Anna replied with confidence and a slight smile—but still, a smile.

"The morn ye go to school. Feelin' this well, you should be there…with your friends," her mum said with some firmness.

"OK, OK, Mummy. I promise," Anna said while rolling her eyes.

Agnes, joking, chased Anna out of the house with a wooden spoon in hand. Agnes and Anna laughed. "Don't you roll your eyes at me, lassie!" Agnes said while running out of breath, laughing as Anna ran out the door. Nancy almost spit out her tea, she was laughing so hard.

"So, what 'this and that' do ye have in store today, Agnes?" Nancy asked with a little bit of fun sarcasm.

"Oh, ye know…a little this and that." Both Nancy and Agnes laughed.

"Always a mystery with you, dear friend. Since I moved across the street ten years ago, we have been best friends. You can trust me," Nancy said with a smirk.

Agnes replied with a bit of hesitation, "It's Druid stuff. I do my prayers to the spirits in the morning. That's all."

"Hmm, if I knew better, there's more, but I'll accept your answer." Nancy made a slight grin, accepting the unvarying Druid answer.

"I was actually going to the co-op to get ingredients for clootie dumplings. Most importantly, contact that doctor in Glasgow for Anna. Dr. Glen Stone, I think his name was. I just hope he's not the type to give prescriptions to turn Anna comatose. Last thing I need to be doin' is putting money in the chemist's pocket," Agnes said with authority.

"Did you want company?" Nancy asked hesitantly.

"Sure. I just need to get proper ready. You don't mind waitin', love?" Agnes asked with kindness in her voice.

"Of course not. I might drink up all this lovely tea while I wait," Nancy said with a giddy smile. "On second thought, let me freshen up a bit and you can pick me up when you're ready," Nancy said.

"Brilliant, Nancy. I'll ring ye when I'm on my way," Agnes said.

"OK, see ye in a bit, love," Nancy said with a smile and a wave. Her hair was still tossed about from the wee hours before.

Agnes finished being finicky in the kitchen and headed upstairs to get ready for the day.

The temperature that day was fourteen degrees, and it was just too cold to wear a dress. She put on black trousers and a red blouse with white and red lilies, black pumps, and ruby-red stud earrings that Anna had made for her. Agnes gazed into the long oval mirror, thinking to herself, *Oh, how the time has come and gone.* She remembered when she and Thomas had first gotten married. Agnes had been slender, standing a straight 169 centimeters, with soft wavy light-brown hair and hazel eyes. She was always wearing soft-pink lipstick. She pictured Thomas sitting on the edge of the bed, looking at her with a huge smile.

"You always look lovely, my darling." Remembering his words brought a smile to her face. It wasn't just how she looked with him; it was her heart he had loved the most.

❧

Nancy got settled, putting on her seat belt.

"You look so chipper now," Agnes said with a little bit of bewilderment.

"Hubby called in a sickie, and well, do I need to say more?" Nancy said with a cheeky grin.

"Oh my! You sure you want to hang out with me, then?" Agnes said, grinning and all wide-eyed.

"Oh, I'm sure. Ahem, there will be more later," Nancy said with a naughty giggle.

"Nancy! We may have to stop by the church if you keep that up!" Agnes said, shocked. Both of them laughed.

Agnes pulled into the co-op and grabbed a trolley, placing her reusable bags in it. Agnes and Nancy went down each aisle because Agnes had forgotten her list, as usual.

"Let me guess, you forgot your list," Nancy said.

"Well, I have a lot on my mind, ye know," Agnes said with a sigh. Agnes changed the subject quickly by focusing on the ingredients she needed. She continued. "Now, I don't want to add so many different fruits. That makes it nasty, like the gross concoction of the American fruitcake. Have you ever tasted such a thing, Nancy?" Agnes asked with a disgusted look on her face.

"Cannae say I have," Nancy replied.

"Good! A life saved. Mine will have only cranberries," Agnes confirmed.

Just then, William approached.

"Mrs. Aird, Ms. Nancy, how are you?" William asked politely, giving a slight bow.

"Hello, William, we're doing fine. Why aren't ye in school, laddie? Everything all right?" Agnes asked with concern.

"Yes and no. Ms. Nancy, I heard about your attack early this morn from James. He seems fine, but I can tell he's a bit shaken up," William said cautiously. He stood 185 centimeters and was slender yet buff, with hazel eyes and light-brown wavy hair.

"James didn't like the fact he had to go to school, but thank you for looking after him," Nancy said with appreciation. William looked at Agnes with slight intimidation and asked, "Have you seen Anna, Mrs. Aird?"

"She's down by the quarry, love," Agnes said. In the back of her mind, she knew that William was smitten with her Anna. Ever since they had become friends three years ago, he had always looked out for her. William was closer to eighteen and was respectful in every way and well proper when he needed to be but fun also. Always crackin' a joke or two around Anna. It was probably why Anna cared for him so much.

"Thank you, Mrs. Aird," William said.

"When you find her, make sure she gets home relatively early please, love," Agnes said politely.

"Of course, Mrs. Aird," William said.

"OK, laddie. You know you can call me Mum!" Agnes said with a slight grin.

William walked away with a huge smile.

"Now, that lad there is top notch. He's a good one there," she said, then leaned over to Nancy. "Good one for my Anna," Agnes said with a proud smile. Nancy smiled and nodded her head in agreement.

"What time is it?" Agnes asked.

"Half twelve," Nancy replied.

"Oh, good. Let's get out of here and get a bite to eat," Agnes said, pushing her trolley faster.

"Sounds brilliant," Nancy said. Just then her stomach growled. "I guess I am hungry," Nancy said with an embarrassed chuckle.

They got to the checkout, and Agnes unloaded her bags and messages on the conveyor. Nancy noticed the cashier glaring at Agnes.

"Agnes," Nancy whispered. When Agnes looked at Nancy inquisitively, Nancy's eyes widened, and she nodded to inform Agnes to look at the cashier. The name on the blue-and-white plastic name tag was Jacquelyn. The young girl was still glaring in between scanning the messages.

"Lass, you're glarin'. Are you all right?" Agnes asked with concern and authority.

Nancy covered her eyes in a way as if to say, "Oh, shite, here we go." One thing about Agnes was that she could be sweet and selfless yet bold as a Viking when she felt attacked.

"I'm fine!" Jacquelyn snapped sarcastically.

"Right. Well, you might want to smile and act polite before someone jumps over this counter and grabs you by the back of the neck!" Agnes snapped back. Without Nancy or anyone else noticing, her eyes glowed a dim yellow while she glared at Jacquelyn.

Jacquelyn's eyes were as big as cue balls. She replied, "Yes, ma'am."

Nancy helped carry the groceries to the car. Agnes was pretty quiet on the way to Nana's Chips. This eatery was wedged between a pharmacy and a bakery along a narrow, curved road on the B706. Two large bay windows were in the front with a large black door between them. As they walked in, Mrs. McConnell was very happy to welcome them and seat them straightaway.

"Here ye go, ladies. Your server will be out shortly," Mrs. McConnell said with a bright smile.

"Thank you," Nancy and Agnes said.

"I haven't been here in such a long time. They seem to have upgraded. Look at these wooden tables and chairs! So shiny, as though they were made by hand, like we did here many decades ago," Nancy said. Mrs. McConnell put the pair in the back corner. Oddly, the eatery was not too crowded as of yet.

"Ye, these are very nice. I'm impressed," Agnes stated, giving a look of approval of the new designs.

A young waitress emerged and gently placed the water and proper silverware on the table and handed each of them a menu.

"Hello, ladies. How are you today?" she asked with a bright smile.

"Doing quite well, lass," Agnes replied.

"I'll be back momentarily to take your order," she stated and left with a mild skip in her step.

"I'm glad our town is starting to bustle again. It is as though the curse has been lifted. You're a Druid; you must feel some change in the air," Nancy said optimistically.

"Och, there's definitely a change in the air, that's for sure," Agnes replied.

"OK, spill it! What was that all about at the store? Why did she seem upset with you?" Nancy asked.

"It's not something I can discuss here. People have apparently developed sonic hearing whenever I'm around," Agnes stated, rolling her eyes.

"I have a distinct feeling you know more than what you portray. What are you hiding?" Nancy asked as she squinted her eyes.

"What are you accusing me of?" Agnes asked in a whispering growl.

"You have had encounters that no one else has with other Druids—or other people, for that matter—and I feel

you know more about the shadows"—Nancy paused—
"and the missing or hidden altar," she whispered. Nancy
also didn't want to draw attention as she knew if she did,
it's likely the shadow would return to torment her family.
Agnes looked at her friend at first with heartless disdain.
*How dare she question her? How dare she assume I have all
the answers!*

"Nancy, my dear friend, like I mentioned before, I
will tell you what I know. But not here," Agnes stated
quietly yet firmly.

There was a heavy silence between Nancy and Agnes,
and Nancy had to do something to break the ice.

"How is Sabrina liking Edinburgh?" Nancy asked.

"She's really liking it. After Thomas was taken, she
just became mute, as you know. She's doing outstanding
in school and has lots of friends. Thank God Irene took
her in for us. I miss her something fierce," Agnes said,
frowning.

"When do you think you'll be able to visit her?"
Nancy asked.

"Hopefully soon. When we talk, it seems like she
doesn't want to talk to any of us. Not that we did anything wrong, just that we remind her of what the shadows
have done. To her father, her friends. Oh my, speaking
of which, I need to call that Dr. Stone in Glasgow to set
up an appointment. I'll do that now," Agnes said. Agnes
pulled out her iPhone33 and dialed the number from a
small piece of paper.

"Good afternoon, how may I direct your call?" the
operator asked.

"Dr. Stone's office, please," Agnes responded.

"One moment, please," the operator said.

"Good afternoon, Dr. Stone's office. How may I help you?" the receptionist asked.

"Yes, I would like to get my daughter, Anna, into an appointment, please. We are from Beith, and I'm afraid the shadows have deeply affected her," Agnes said anxiously.

"Let me check. Well, you are in luck! We had a cancellation for tomorrow. How does nine a.m. sound?" the receptionist asked.

"Sounds absolutely perfect," Agnes responded happily.

"Can I get your name, please?" she asked.

"I'm Agnes Aird, but my daughter is Anna," Agnes stated.

"Very well. We do ask you arrive a bit early to fill out a few forms, but Anna is scheduled for tomorrow morning at nine a.m. We will see you then," the receptionist said.

"Thank you very much. Take care," Agnes stated as she ended the call. She continued talking to Nancy. "Well, easy enough. The appointment is for tomorrow at nine a.m. You comin' with us?" Agnes asked.

"Sure. It would be nice to hear a doctor's perspective. What time are we leaving?" Nancy asked.

"With normal traffic and hopefully no maintenance on the road, we can leave around eight a.m.," Agnes said plainly.

"That sounds good. I'll be there," Nancy said.

The bubbly waitress returned to take their order.

"Hello, ladies. What can I get for ye?"

"Oh dear. We were too busy chatting," Agnes said as she hastily looked through the menu. "Ah, I'll have the haddock supper, please, lass."

"What dressing would you like on your salad?" she asked.

"Italian is fine, love," Agnes replied, giving a gentle smile.

"Oh, and what would you like to drink?" she asked.

"Just nonbubbly water," Agnes replied.

"And for you, ma'am?" The waitress looked over toward Nancy.

"I'll have the king rib supper, please, with Italian dressing on the salad, and Irn-Bru, please," Nancy replied.

"OK, I'll go ahead and get that order in," she said with a smile as she darted toward the kitchen.

"I'm hoping Anna is home when I get there," Agnes said. She grabbed a notebook and pen out of her large purse. Nancy looked at her inquisitively. Agnes then wrote in the notebook, *I was high priestess by default*. Nancy looked at her in shock.

"What do you mean?" Nancy whispered.

Agnes went back to the notebook and wrote, *The spirits didn't give her fire nor ice in the chalice when she was made high priestess, so it was voted on from the grove.*

"Why are you telling me this?" Nancy asked quietly.

"Because you wanted to know why the cashier, Jacquelyn, was giving me the glare." Agnes then wrote in her notebook, *We haven't done much because what powers I do have to call upon the spirits are just enough to convince the grove I am worthy enough to be a high priestess.*

Nancy grabbed the pen and wrote in the notebook, *You really don't know where the altar is then.*

Agnes hesitated for a moment before responding. Could she really trust Nancy with her secret? Or did she have to lie in order to save the grove? Agnes took the pen and wrote, *Correct.*

"I guess I don't know much about all this Druid stuff and what anyone can do or can't do. However, I will admit, I have speculated for many years that you were lying and keeping secrets," Nancy said. She had a frown on her face and sat sluggishly in her seat as though a mountain of guilt had been placed on her shoulders.

"Many people have been making those speculations, and I must keep the grove in harmony, or we may not have a grove at all! These young Druids are trying to find their way and understand their place within the grove. Most of them are teens. Could you imagine a teen running a grove?" Agnes asked, giving a look of disbelief just thinking about a teen being head of a grove. "It's nonsense!" Agnes exclaimed.

"I can understand completely. Some decisions are difficult to make and keep at the same time. You are trying to do your best for your grove," Nancy said politely.

"Well, I thank you for your understanding," Agnes said in a polite yet direct manner. She had to find a way to keep Nancy at bay until she could figure out what was going on with Anna. The shadow seemed to be picking up momentum in finding new victims. For fifty years, deaths had usually numbered one to two every other year; however, the shadow seems unsettled, as though it is losing its dominance over Beith. Deaths were more like one to two every year now. Agnes didn't know how long she could keep up her charade of being a barely powerful high priestess.

Agnes wasn't thrilled about telling Nancy part of her secret, but something had to be said to buy some time until she found a way to suppress the shadow.

"How was everything?" the waitress asked. She softly placed the check on the table.

"Delightful. Thank you, lass," Agnes replied.

"You can pay up at the register once you are ready," the waitress said.

"Thank you, love," Nancy replied.

The young waitress headed back to the kitchen while Nancy and Agnes finished up their meals.

"Well, that was good. Let's get home before the food spoils. Plus, I fear something is wrong with Anna," Agnes said anxiously.

"I'm sure she's fine, but you'll drive me crazy until you are where you need to be," Nancy said as she rolled her eyes somewhat jokingly with Agnes. Nancy snatched the check from the table.

"Sneaky devil, you woman!" Agnes said. They both laughed and headed to the register. Nancy knew once Agnes made up her mind about what she needed to do, there was no changing it.

The receptionist called Dr. Stone to inform him of his early appointment.

"Yes?"

"You have a nine a.m. appointment with an Anna Aird. She comes from Beith, and her mother seems concerned about her well-being," the receptionist explained.

"Hmm." Dr. Stone gave a sigh, and the receptionist interrupted him.

"Dr. Stone, I understand that you want to help the community of Beith, but maybe this next client will give you the answers you need," the receptionist said with a bit of enthusiasm.

"Thank you, for your concern. We can only hope," Dr. Stone stated as he hung up the phone. He rubbed his head, wishing his headache would go away. He reached into the top right drawer of his desk, pulled out a packet of Doyle's headache powder, and dumped the contents into a shot of whisky. He leaned back in his luxurious chair and put his feet on the desk. It wasn't for another hour that his next client would arrive. His personal mobile rang, and the screen said, *Unknown number*. He reluctantly clicked the green answer button.

"Hello," Dr. Stone answered.

"Don't get too comfortable," the mystery man stated. Dr. Stone jumped up and looked frantically out the window. The mystery man continued. "You still need to find the one who will suppress me. If not, you die."

"I haven't forgotten," Dr. Stone said with a shaky voice. The call disconnected. Then a text came in giving him a number to call when he found the one. Whatever whisky he'd had in his body, his body had burned off its effect after the call.

Chapter 5

THE MESSAGE

Anna reached the west side of the quarry. Most of the leaves had fallen from the rich-smelling birch trees, and within the leaves, the squirrels would play. However, this particular day seemed perceptibly quiet. The birds were not singing, and the atmosphere had an unearthly feeling of dread. Anna ignored it and headed to her normal gem location. She knew that was where the best jewels were. Anna often wondered how the crystals and gems continued to form here after all this time. She would often ponder whether it was something scientific or whether the water was just simply magical. Being fifteen years old, she concluded in her mind that it was scientific because she was too old now for faerie tales.

She reached the wooded area and noticed an older woman washing clothes. Anna had been here for months, and not until today had she seen this woman or a wooden shack. The shack was surrounded by a heavy layer of mist that crept towards them. It was a one-story building of decaying and warped wood. It appeared as though the structure had been there for decades. White smoke flowed from the chimney on the right side. At first glance, there were only two long windows, one on each side of the front door. Surrounding the shack stood lengthy, tall dead trees with ravens, at least six in each, as though they protected the area by force. As Anna moved closer to the strange woman, the ravens gawked, eyeing Anna as though they were ready to attack.

"Don't mind them, lass. They are my pets," the strange crone said with her old, witchy, crackling voice.

Anna felt an instant flush of fear come over her and didn't want to be rude, yet she wanted to escape quickly.

"I smell your fear. I'm just an old lady who loves being part of nature," the crone said. Then there was a pause. The older woman continued washing her clothes. Anna caught glimpses of what she was cleaning and red bleeding onto the old washboard. The older woman looked up at Anna. Anna could see the few remaining black rotted teeth as the woman said in her crackling voice, "I'm just washing the blood from your father's shirt."

Anna gasped. Her heart started racing, and she now felt she was in absolute danger. Anna went to turn and run, but the second Anna turned around, the old crone was directly in front of her. Anna's eyes widened as she looked at the older woman.

"You wear the mark, child," the older woman said.

"What mark? Who are you really? I have been coming here for months and never seen this shack, or you for that matter! And why do you have my father's shirt? How do you know him?" Anna demanded. Her voice was shaking, and she needed answers now!

"In due time, child, you will have your answers. Be wary of what surrounds you as those dangers are why Beith carries the curse. Only those that bear the mark have the power to seal the curse's fate," the older woman said.

She then walked steadily toward the shack, opened the door, and walked inside without looking back. The door gently closed. Anna stood there and watched the woman disappear. She needed answers to the riddles the woman had given her. Anna then got a determined look and marched to the shack. As she got closer, the ravens cawed louder and louder as she approached the door.

"Ma'am! Ma'am!" Anna said while desperately knocking on the door. "Ma'am, I still have questions. Can I come in?" Anna asked hesitantly.

The door opened on its own, and when it was open completely, Anna looked bewildered, as she saw nothing inside. It was one room. There was no wood in the fireplace, yet smoke still flowed upward. Anna ran back to the quarry, but the washboard was gone. Anna stood at the quarry in disbelief.

Behind the house, the old woman was walking in the opposite direction. The farther the old woman got away from the shack, the more she transformed into a young lady with flowing long brown hair and bright-blue eyes; she was slender, with many freckles on her nose and cheeks. The once-old crone, now a young lady, had to get a message out to Anna but wasn't sure how.

Meanwhile, Anna got on her bike and headed straight home. She raced home as though nighttime was closing in, even though it was only midday. She constantly looked behind her, making sure nothing was following her. Anna zipped up the driveway, slammed her bike down onto the ground, not even noticing the groundskeepers, and ran to her room.

Anna looked at the clock, and it was only 11:10 a.m. She regretted not going to school now, yet all she could think about was what the mysterious old crone had been trying to tell her. What did she mean, *Only those that bear the mark can seal the curse's fate? Who else bears the mark if the curse is over fifty years old? Do I have the power to lift the curse?* Anna boggled her brain with questions, giving herself no viable answers. She got into her bed and snuggled under her duvet. Anna thought it might protect her from any possible evils around her.

She fell into a deep sleep and started to dream. At first, it was very dark; the light flickered from candles on pillars around a small altar. A figure in a black cloak, black robe, and black gloves stood at the altar, chanting quietly and repeating, *Um sum al tomb matra diem Direal.* The figure in the black cloak said the chant three times, and after the third time, a shadowy figure appeared. It was the exact figure that had taken her father.

Anna's body began to twitch, and her eyes shifted back and forth rapidly.

"Why do you call upon me?" the shadow figure asked sternly.

"I, Nixia, daughter of the dark king, have come to warn you, Direal. The one that bears your mark will be your demise," Nixia said.

"How dare you summon me here!" Direal stated. His voice tried to cover hers.

"Silence! I have the power to damn you to the nether-world. Do not underestimate me. I came as a favour, but now, your warning will soon be your death," Nixia said, and then she turned into a crow and flew away. Direal turned as though he was looking straight at Anna.

"I'm coming for you," Direal stated as he pointed toward Anna, and the dark shadow came closer to her.

Anna jumped up from her slumber and had a shocked look on her face. She was sweating profusely, as though she had come out of a burning inferno. She looked at her arm, noticed it was glowing red, and started to cry, wondering why this was happening to her. After a few moments, the glowing dissipated, and only the symbol remained. Typically, the scar would look like a scratch after the glowing stopped. This time, it was different. The symbol had a lotus with a triangle on the top and bottom, with the points facing the lotus. At the base of each triangle, centered, was a diamond and an arrow pointing away from the lotus.

Anna needed the pain to stop! She needed to figure out if she was the cause or the solution to Beith's curse.

"Sari, look up this symbol," Anna said. Sari (Sarr-ree) was an AI research "brain" inside a significant database. It had replaced the early Siri due to hackers manipulating the database and having over £1.6M worth of jewelry sent to a different residence. When that failed, the jewelry had ended up at multiple homes throughout East Ayrshire. The hackers had never been found, nor the millions of pounds' worth of jewelry. Because of this massive security breach, Sari had been born.

After a few seconds, Sari responded, "This symbol is called the Lucid Protector symbol. This symbol was last seen in the late 1600s to protect children from witches. It has also been used in the Druid community, and similar runes exist for protection against evil. Do you require additional information?"

"No," Anna said. Sari then turned off. Anna was confused. She was trying to piece together what the crone had said and what the dream meant—and now a protection rune? Anna couldn't wait until her mum got home so she could potentially get some answers.

William got down to the quarry, and there was no sign of Anna. He searched around the usual spot, and no Anna. William started to panic and called out to her. "Anna! Anna!" But there was no response. He went into the line of trees, and some ravens gawked as he moved through the small wood line, but nothing. He looked into the water to see if maybe one of her mining tools had fallen into the water, but still nothing. Then there was a snap. William looked behind him, and an old man stood by the water.

"You scared me, sir," William said as he gasped for air with his hand over his heart.

"Sorry, lad. I heard some yellin' and came straight over. Everything all right?" the old man asked with concern.

"My Anna was supposed to be here looking for her crystals, but she's not. Have you seen her, sir?" William asked in desperation.

"Anna? I know Anna, but I have not seen her diggin' about today. Is she back at school?" the old man asked inquisitively. "Excuse my manners, I'm Mr. Galloway from the house just down the way there," he said.

"I'm William, sir. Glad to make your acquaintance," William said politely.

"You're a proper lad. Please, call me Michael," he said.

"Right, Michael, OK then," William said awkwardly. He had been brought up to be very respectful and formal to elders. To be anything else was considered insolent.

"Say, do you think you can help me with something? I need some wood moved to the shed near my home," Michael asked humbly. Michael, was stocky and yet muscular, stood roughly 177 centimeters, had a full head of gray hair, and wore round-rimmed glasses. He had a little belly, but being sixty-two, he could look any way he wanted.

"Sure," William said hesitantly.

"Don't worry, lad, I'll give you a good wage for your help," Michael said with a soft smile. "It's the least I could do after keeping you away from finding Anna. I'm sure she's probably at home safe, lad," Michael said with certainty.

William looked back one last time, but no Anna. The older man was perhaps correct. There was nothing to worry about, and Anna was probably safe at home. William wasn't exactly wearing work clothes, but he gave his word to help. Michael had been chopping wood since early morning, and five piles of wood needed to be consolidated in the shed already.

Michael continued to chop wood as William stored it. He carried four pieces at a time from the pile of fifteen— each piece stacked with the cut edge facing down.

"Need some water, lad?" Michael asked.

"Yes, please," William replied. He gulped the water down and went back to stacking the wood.

After about an hour, William stated, "All finished, Michael."

"Well done, lad. Thank you so much. Here's a hundred pounds for your troubles," Michael said as he handed William a crisp £100 note.

"Thank you so much, sir. I mean, Michael," William said ecstatically.

"Go find Anna. And you are welcome back anytime. Well, not for work, but you are welcome at my home whenever you and Anna like," Michael said.

"Thank you. Take care," William said as he rushed off to Anna's house. Michael smiled.

William drove to Anna's house as fast as legally possible. He arrived at her house at 12:30 p.m. William knocked on the door but didn't want to seem too frantic. Anna had already been startled by her dream and was hesitant even to move. William knocked louder this time.

"Anna, it's me! William!" William yelled anxiously. He paced back and forth, putting his hands through this hair. Anna, hearing him, ran downstairs and opened the door.

"William, hi. Sorry, I was upstairs," Anna said, trying not to portray that anything was wrong.

"I saw your mum with Ms. Nancy at the co-op earlier, and she asked me to ensure you were safe. I got scared when I didn't see you at the quarry," William explained.

"Scared? Over me?" Anna asked with a perplexed look. William rolled his eyes.

"Yes, Anna, you know I care deeply for you," William said as he gently caressed her shoulders. Anna's eyes widened, and she blushed. William slowly pulled Anna toward him, his eyes passionately looking into Anna's. They both closed their eyes, and their lips embraced their first kiss. Anna put her arms against his chest, then slowly moved them around his neck. William put one hand behind her back and the other behind her head. The kiss wasn't a kiss of friendship. William and Anna fell in love. Their kiss lasted a few moments, but after, William gently moved his hand across her soft, rosy cheeks and, with loving conviction, said, "Anna, I love you. I will wait however long it takes to be with you."

"I love you as well, but you may not after you hear about what happened to me today," Anna said sarcastically. She continued. "I don't want to burden you with such nonsense."

"Anna, I know you have been dealing with a lot since the demon took your father. I swear, I'm here for you; I'm not going anywhere," William said with purpose. He was determined to keep her trust no matter how crazy things seemed in her life. Anna started pulling splinters from William's jumper.

"I'll explain that after you tell me about your morning," he stated.

"Well." She paused. "Wait, you said you went to the quarry today? Did you see an old woman and a shack in the wood line?" she asked in desperation. William looked at her oddly.

"You promised!" Anna yelled.

"You're right, you're right. Sorry. No, I didn't see anything. What did you see?" William asked. He was now intently focused on Anna.

"Ever since this scratch turned into a symbol, a protection rune, weird things have been happening to me. Like today, I went to the quarry and noticed smoke from the tree line. There was a shack, as though it had been there for ages. Then an old woman was washing some bloody clothes. She spoke in riddles, which totally annoyed me, saying that I will find out things in due time and that I bear the mark. When I followed her back to her shack, the place was empty. Oh, and the shirt she was washing was my dad's," Anna explained. She was talking so fast it wasn't comprehensible.

"Slow down, Anna. OK, so when you went to the quarry this morning, some old lady was washing your father's shirt, there was a shack, and she said your scar was the mark of some dude? Please tell me I'm close," William said, trying to sort out what he had just heard.

"Yes. Exactly!" Anna exclaimed. William sighed in relief, and then Anna looked at him strangely.

"OK, your turn," Anna said.

"There was an elderly man, Michael Galloway, who saw me at the quarry. He asked if I could help put chopped wood away in a shed. He was nice, but something seemed off about him," William said but with uncertainty about Mr. Galloway.

"Hmm, I've never met him. Maybe he is just lonely," Anna replied with optimism.

"That's odd. Mr. Galloway said he knew you," William retorted.

"Maybe he said that because he has always seen me there," Anna said.

"Maybe. Anyway, Mr. Galloway did give me a hundred quid for helping him," William said with a smile.

"That's great! What are you getting me?" Anna said as she laughed.

"Well, you have me. That should be enough, right?" William asked while being funny.

"Hardly!" Anna exclaimed. William was in shock, then he started tickling and kissing her.

"Anything else I should know?" William asked while they went to sit in the living room. He put his arms around her and again focused on her.

"Well, it was bizarre. It was like I was in the background of a meeting. This person in all black was chanting something and summoned this demon. The one that looked like the one that took my dad. They got into a brief argument. I can't remember what was being said, but then it was as though he was pointing at me and said, 'I'm coming for you!'" Anna expressed with fear.

William's eyes widened, and he held her tighter. "Wow! That sounds scary." He then rubbed Anna's back to comfort her.

"I just have so many questions: Who else has borne this mark? Why did it seem like the crone at the quarry was trying to warn me? How can this be the mark of Direal but a rune of protection? Has a demon branded me? Am I the link to the curse?" Anna asked these questions out loud while streams of tears flowed down her face. She looked withdrawn and full of uncertainty. Anna started staring off into the distance, then looked at the mark and gently rubbed it with her fingers. She cuffed her hand over it completely and let out a long sigh.

"William, will you help me solve this mystery? There has got to be a connection between this mark and the curse," Anna said with enthusiasm. She turned to face William, took him by his shoulders, and asked, "What say you?"

"Of course! I was just thinking about something, but you have to promise not to get mad," William said hesitantly.

"OK," Anna said, raising one eyebrow.

"There is no way that no one knows why this town is cursed. The Druid altars were placed decades ago, and your mother is a high priestess," William said sternly.

"What are you suggesting, William? My mother is behind all this?" Anna asked angrily.

"I am just saying, love, a high priestess doesn't know how to 'talk to the spirits' to find the altar? Seems a little odd." William paused, shrugged his shoulders, and made a peculiar face, raising his eyebrows, his eyes a little wide and lips tight together to indicate Anna might want to start asking her mum questions.

"If anything, she would be trying to protect the grove. I'm not into all that, but the spirits made her the high priestess, so they must have known what they were doing," Anna said.

"Well, all I'm saying is you might want to have a proper chat with your mum," William said.

Just then, the door swung open, and it was Agnes and Ms. Nancy.

"Impeccable timing," William said as he and Anna got up from the couch.

"William. Anna. Could you please get the rest of the messages from the car, please?" Agnes asked as she started emptying the bags she had brought in.

"Sure," William said. He nudged Anna to talk to her mum.

"OK. Ugh!" Anna responded. Anna vacillated but still moved closer to her mum.

"Mum. I need to talk to you. It's vital," Anna said.

"You're shaking, child! What is it?" Agnes proclaimed, but at the same time, she tried to comfort her.

"Mum, look!" She rolled up her sleeve and showed her the rune that now replaced the scratch that had once been there. Agnes grabbed her arm and looked at the rune with amazement.

"How long has this been on you?" Agnes asked with concern. Her eyes opened wide at first, but then she looked at Anna seriously. "Do you have any idea what this is?" Agnes asked profoundly.

"I don't know.. I checked on the computer, and it's a protection rune," Anna responded. Anna could tell something was wrong by her mother's face.

"Yes, it's a protection rune, but who put that on you?"

"It just showed up recently. I swear!" Anna proclaimed.

"OK, OK, calm down," Agnes said as she tried to figure out what to do next.

"Tell her what you told me," William said.

"Tell me what?" Agnes asked. She was becoming increasingly scared of the situation.

Anna looked back at William, then looked at her mum.

"There was an old crone in the woods by the quarry today. She was washing Dad's shirt, which had bloodstains on it. The crone's house had ravens around it, but when I went to the house, she disappeared. She told me I bear the mark and answers to my questions would come in due time. Then I had a bad dream where this lady in a black robe was threatening this demon named Direal, and when I woke up, the rune on my arm started glowing red," Anna said as she started to cry. Agnes grabbed her and held her tight.

"I am so sorry you are going through this! Good thing you have an appointment tomorrow with Dr. Stone in Glasgow. I'm sure he will be able to come up with something to help," Agnes stated. She continued gently. "Are you sure you didn't imagine all this? You have been under so much stress since your father died."

"No! I swear, Mum! That crone was down there! But when I returned to the quarry after coming from the shack, the washboard was gone, along with Dad's shirt," Anna said. William was holding her now.

"Anything else go on?" Agnes asked. By this time, Agnes was just distraught.

"I ran into someone that you might know. His name was Michael Galloway," William said.

"Mr. Galloway. Old man from the east side of the quarry?" Agnes asked with confusion.

"I believe so. Mr. Galloway asked if I could help him put chopped wood in the shed. He gave me a hundred quid for it." William smiled.

"Show me this money," Agnes demanded.

William took out his wallet and showed her the hundred-pound note. Agnes was surprised to see that they were legit notes. She looked at William and proceeded to tell him, "Mr. Galloway has been dead for three years now," Agnes said calmly.

Nancy finished unpacking the groceries and mumbled to herself, "Here we go with the weird shit again." Agnes was pleased to see the messages put away.

"Thank you so much, Nancy. You are such a dear, dear friend. What would I do without you?" Agnes said in a humble way.

"That's a very good question. Now, are we heading to the quarry?" Nancy said authoritatively.

"You read my mind," Agnes said.

"OK, you two, get in the car while there is still daylight," Agnes said as she scooted everyone out the door.

They reached Kilburn Loch by Mulch Water. Anna showed them the sandy area where she had gone to get the gems and seen the crone.

"Where is the shack you saw?" Nancy asked.

"Straight through here." Anna pointed. Then they started to walk that way.

Everyone followed Anna as she led the charge. Anna stopped.

"Well, it was here, but it's all birch trees," Anna said in disappointment.

"However, where the shack was, all those ravens still remain. What do you think it means, Mum?" Anna asked.

"Well, just through here is Mr. Galloway's house," William stated excitedly.

Agnes stood still and didn't say a word. Nancy looked at Agnes as she knew Agnes might understand what had transpired. Agnes started walking toward William's direction of Mr. Galloway's house. When they all reached the house, it was as though it had been abandoned for a while. William ran over toward the shed where he had placed the wood earlier and opened it. His eyes darted back and forth in amazement, checking each shelf.

"Look at this! The wood is still fresh! As if someone had just cut it today. Hmm, imagine that," William said sarcastically.

"Let's go knock on the door. Maybe someone new lives here," Agnes said.

When William approached the front door, the two steps that led to the porch creaked, the porch swing swayed by its rusted chains, and small dead tree limbs adorned the door. He then tried looking into a window with his hands cupped around his face.

"I don't see anyone," William said. He continued. "However, he did say we could come by at any time."

"Are you sure this is the house?" Anna asked. Her arms were folded, and she was also displaying a smug look. She was frustrated thinking no one had believed her, and now they were wasting their time at some dead man's house.

"Yes, I'm sure!" William snapped back.

"See if the door is unlocked," Anna suggested.

"Oh, brilliant idea. Let's just break in to someone's house," William said cynically.

"Well, it's better than standing here waiting for the shadow to get us," Anna said, returning the sarcasm.

"Fine!" William said. He turned the old-style brass doorknob. The door was unlocked. William pushed the door open and yelled out, "Hello! Hello! Mr. Galloway? Are you here? It's William."

They stood in the front room where an old round wooden table with four chairs stood. There was a window to the right surrounded by family pictures and paintings of Scottish castles.

"This is him!" William exclaimed. It was a picture of Mr. Galloway and an old friend showing off their catch of the day.

"Hmm, that looks like Lester Mucky from down the road. If I remember correctly, I think he is still around and lives just up the road from here," Agnes said affirmatively.

The house wasn't in any disarray and was quite orderly. Just the way he had left it when the shadow took him three years ago. Anna looked at some of the books lying on the coffee table in front of the two couches. There was an old leather book with no title and a bright-orange tab sticking out of a particular page. She opened the book to the page and saw a picture of a rune that closely matched the rune on her arm.

"Mum! Look at this! It's the rune on my arm!" Anna said ecstatically.

"I don't think Mr. Galloway will mind you having this," Agnes said. She gave Anna a nod, giving her approval to take the book.

"Let's go, laddie. Let's see if Mr. Mucky is home," Agnes said.

They made it to Mr. Mucky's house and inquired about Mr. Galloway. He confirmed that he had died three years ago and that Mr. Mucky has been trying to keep up the house.

"Do you know anything about this book, sir?" Anna asked.

Mr. Mucky looked at the book and recognised it straightaway.

"Ah, very much so. Michael spent the last part of his life trying to find ways to protect himself from the shadow. It was as if he was trying to turn himself into a self-made warlock or something. But please. Keep it. I have no use for it, and I think he wouldn't mind you having it," Mr. Mucky assured Anna with a smile.

"Well, we won't waste any more of your time," Agnes said politely.

"No worries at all, Agnes. Please don't hesitate to come by if you have any other questions," Mr. Mucky said.

"I think Mr. Galloway wanted us to find this book for Anna," William declared.

"I think you're right, laddie," Agnes said.

Back at Mr. Galloway's house, Michael's spirit stood by the round wooden table and proclaimed, "My work is done," his last words as he faded away.

Chapter 6

HISTORY LESSON

"It's about time you got here, mate!" Jeremy said as Daniel walked into school. Daniel strolled through the double doors as though he were the prince and his subjects were waiting for his grand entrance.

"I have arrived!" Daniel exclaimed.

"Hurry up, you goof, we have to get to class!" Christian stated.

Daniel, Jeremy, Christian, and Don scurried to their third class, history. Not the local favorite, considering that history focused on the war and nothing other than that.

"Come along, gentlemen. Get in your seats, please," Mrs. Swain said with a slight grin.

Rebecca Swain was slender, properly poised, and wore only professional yet stylish suits. She had long wavy reddish-brown hair and hazel eyes, and she wore glasses only to read. The students loved her because she wanted to understand the youth of the day. The students felt this was authentic and had silently accepted her. The bell rang, and Principal Byington appeared on the monitor above Mrs. Swain's desk.

"Good morning. Ah, yah, so we got the king thing going on next month, you know about that. I have decided that we will have a Ceilidh dance with festivities this year at the end of the month," he said.

Many of the students were very confused. The threat of the shadow meant they couldn't be out in hours of darkness. Yet throughout the school, cheers and screams of excitement echoed through the hallways. Laurie came in late while the chatter was going on.

"What is everyone going on about?" Laurie asked.

"The principal is allowing a dance! Can you believe it?" Daniel said with utter enthusiasm. "And I think I know who I'm going to ask to the dance," Daniel said with a smirk.

"Oh really?" Laurie questioned in a cheeky way and with a huge smile, giving Daniel a kiss.

"OK, settle down, lads and lassies. Listen up!" Mrs. Swain exclaimed with authority.

Mr. Byington continued. "So it sounds like all of you are excited about that. There will be some dance committee thing after school in the sports room with senior class leader Jessica Reed. Oh, and just a reminder, folks, Beith is still under a curse and let's make sure we are watching over each other. Have a wonderful day!" Mr. Byington concluded.

There was chatter from the students already discussing their plans. What to wear? Who was going to ask whom to the dance? A frenzy erupted, and a good one at that! A dance was exactly what the town needed.

Mrs. Swain didn't waste any time getting back into the lesson. Plans for the dance would have to wait.

"OK, OK. We all have seen death and experienced the pain of what the curse has brought us. So now what? Are we going to continue to suffer?" Mrs. Swain asked rhetorically yet seriously. Mrs. Swain wanted an answer too. She wanted to know why the shadowy demon had taken her husband.

"What can we do about it? No one knows where the altar is. Plus, if someone does find it, will the curse be lifted once it's destroyed?" Laurie asked.

Don sat across the room from Laurie and looked at her inquisitively. He was always the one questioning things or being argumentative, yet he was one of the smartest. Usually, people looked up to him because Don was approachable, knowledgeable, and funny to boot! He wondered if she knew something that the other students did not. *What is she hiding?*

"Yer bum is oot the windae, Laurie. We all know that the curse is lifted when the altar is destroyed. Since King Andrew ordered them to be destroyed, people lived in freedom. At this point, the altar may not be in Beith, but someone is controlling it to curse Beith," Daphne said with conviction. She was not one to participate in class, but today was a little out of the ordinary.

"We need to start a rebellion! A rebellion against the curse. We should be living in peace and not fear! For Scotland!" Jeremy said with enthusiasm.

"OK, calm down there, William Wallace," Christian said jokingly.

Some of the other students giggled as well.

"Lunchtime, we'll meet at the birch tree. We will defeat this curse, once and for all!" Daniel said ecstatically.

Daniel took a breather and glanced over at Laurie. Some strands of coarse gray hair were hanging off one of the sleeves of her sweater.

"You dye your hair now?" Daniel asked. "I found some you missed," he said jokingly.

"Oh. Weird," Laurie said with no emotion. She wondered how remnants of her shapeshifting were left over. Could Direal's trust be diminishing? She took a deep breath and let out a little sigh.

"Are you OK? Yer lookin' a bit peely walley," Daniel said with concern while rubbing Laurie's back.

"Yeah, this whole thing with the curse just freaks me out. But yeah, we have to do something about it. You can definitely count on me for support," Laurie said with a slight smile, hesitant because she knew she would either end up staying as Laurie or as the old crone.

Mrs. Swain had noticed Laurie walking in late. She marked her tardy in the book but didn't say a word.

"I know all your focus now is on the dance and the game. However, I need your focus for the next forty-five minutes, please. Today, we will delve into the curse and how our community has become accustomed to it. Who remembers how Beith succumbed to the curse?" Mrs. Swain asked. "Christian Doyle. What do you think?" she asked as she called upon him to answer.

"It is because King Archibald in 2030 ordered that Druidism would be the main religion. Once King

Andrew was declared king of Scotland, he ordered all altars to be demolished and allowed Christianity, both Catholic and Protestant, back as proper religions. Yet one altar remains, and no one can find it," he answered proudly.

"Excellent, Christian," Mrs. Swain replied.

"Here is a tough question. Do we think the missing altar is here in Beith, or is someone or something controlling us from its location?" Mrs. Swain asked intently.

There was silence for almost two full minutes. Those two minutes felt like ten. Mrs. Swain knew it was a tough question, considering many students had suffered loss because of the curse.

A small voice came from the back of the class. Without raising her hand, Clarissa Mills quietly said, "I think it's near the church on the hill."

Everyone turned around and looked—not necessarily glares but preemptive looks as they listened for clarity.

"We have seen altars torn down in Kilmarnock and Glasgow, but it's odd how we are the only ones still cursed. Someone has to know where the altar is. We do have Druids here. Shall I say Daniel's mother is a high priestess? Maybe she is hiding the altar?" Clarissa said calmly but with a bit of sarcasm.

"How dare you even suggest that, you fookin' nyaff! We have suffered as well! The shadow took my father!" Daniel yelled.

Laurie instantly tried to calm Daniel, but he pushed her away. There was a small gasp and some chatter among the students. Some were wide-eyed in shock.

"Why would anyone want to do that? After fifty years, we are the only ones suffering!" Jeremy snarled.

"I'm sick and tired of hiding in the house at night. I'm tired of having to leave town and spend the night at a friend's outside of Beith just to experience the nightlife," Daniel said with frustration.

Laurie understood Daniel's frustration, and rightly so. Soon, she would have to tell him her secret, the truth; however, that time wasn't now.

"Class, let's take a breath. This is difficult for everyone. Let us try not to accuse anyone as no one has any indication of where it is, as we know," Mrs. Swain stated. Then she proceeded to ask another question. "Why do you suppose people gave up looking for the altar?"

"People assumed all altars were destroyed, and we live with a permanent curse," Jeremy said plainly.

"So, you're saying that everyone just gave up and accepted their fate?" Mrs. Swain retorted.

At that point, no one had a reply or a good reason why citizens didn't take an active role in finding the altar. After citizens had searched for fifty years, the consensus was that Beith was cursed. By the year 2065, the population of Beith went from 9,620 to 7,300. By 2080, just over 6,100. Many families that had grown up there moved to populated areas like Glasgow and even as far north as County Skye.

The bell rang.

"Think about this in your off time and how maybe we can find the altar. Have a great day," Mrs. Swain said as the students left the classroom.

"Laurie, I need to talk to you for a moment," Mrs. Swain said.

"What's up, Mrs. Swain?" Laurie asked.

"You have been late to class all this week. Is everything OK?" Mrs. Swain asked.

"It's Druid stuff," Laurie quickly responded. Then she added, "There is more, but I can't discuss here. You talking about the altar puts you in danger. I gotta go." Laurie quickly ran out the door, tried to find Daniel, and found him waiting for her by her locker. She approached, and they give each other a small kiss. He smiled at her but looked at her with concern.

"What was all that about? You all right?" Daniel asked.

"It was nothing really. Mrs. Swain wanted to know why I've been late this week, and I told her it was Druid stuff. Nothing to be concerned about, but I reassured her I wouldn't be late anymore," Laurie said and gave Daniel a slight smile to say it was not a big deal. She grabbed some books from the locker, and they went to the next class. Daniel felt uneasy because Laurie looked like she was hiding something, and he decided to press the issue.

"How long have we been datin', love?" Daniel asked Laurie.

"About two years. Why?" Laurie raised one eyebrow and gave him an inquiring look.

"So then, you do realize I know when something is off. Have I ever given you any indication that you cannae trust me? You can tell me anything. And if it has to do with Druid stuff, trust me, I hear weird bits from my mum regularly. Nothing you would say would shock me," Daniel said, trying to reassure her.

"Hmm, you say that, but what I know may shock you," she retorted.

"Well, then, I guess you will have to find me under the big birch tree behind the school for lunch today and tell me all about it," Daniel said with jocularity. Laurie smiled and rolled her eyes at him.

"Fine. But you must promise me you can't fly off the handle or get crazy," Laurie demanded.

"Oh my! Sounds juicy! OK, I promise," Daniel said.

"I'm serious, Daniel!" Laurie exclaimed in a softer voice so the whole school didn't inquire about their conversation.

"Fine! OK! I get it! Still. Sounds juicy." Daniel smiled while holding her.

Laurie did a facepalm and responded, "I give up." They gave each other a long kiss, and although Daniel wanted to kiss her interminably, she pushed him away so she could get to class.

Daniel had a free hour before lunch, so he decided to get some Subway and bring it back for him and Laurie. There wouldn't be time to go and hear this extraordinary story Laurie had promised. He lay out a blanket and waited for her. The fourth-hour bell rang, and a few moments later, Laurie was seen walking briskly toward Daniel. He stood up and greeted her with a kiss.

"Oh my god. You got all this? Thank you so much! I totally need this right now!" Laurie said excitedly.

"How did your algebra test go?" Daniel asked and sipped his drink.

"Yikes! I have no idea. I hope it went OK. Like, I think it went well. Fingers crossed," Laurie said with uncertainty.

"Anything else go on?" Daniel asked.

"Not really. A new girl arrived from Glasgow. Latrice something. She seems cool. And of course, the class cheerleader, Judy, showed her around," Laurie said with a slight chuckle.

"To be fair, Judy is charming. She's just happy all the time. With Beith the way it is, we need someone like her around. I'm not complaining," Daniel said plainly.

Laurie started looking around to see who was nearby. The ravens had a habit of spying when the shadow felt like someone was giving out too much information. Thus far, she felt the shadow hadn't seen her transformation act from earlier today.

"OK, you ready? This is going to be serious, and some things you may not understand or believe, but I have to tell you," Laurie stated, sitting close and staring into Daniel's eyes. She started to tremble. She felt that once she told Daniel the truth, they would not be together anymore.

"Goodness, Laurie. Are you OK? I'm here. I promise, no matter what you tell me, good or bad—it sounds like it's going to be both—I'm not going anywhere. You have been there for me, and I may not understand the Druid crap, but I know it's something you're deep into," Daniel reassured Laurie as he caressed her leg and pressed his forehead to hers.

"Here goes nothing." Laurie chuckled slightly, then continued. "Your family has been the catalyst of a curse."

"What? My family?" Daniel exclaimed but in a whisper.

"Hold on, let me finish. I'll lose my train of thought. OK, as I said, your family is likely the cause of the curse. See, I have been away from the grove for quite some time, and even my power of transformation is shady at best. You see, when you saw the gray hair on my sleeve earlier, I knew where your sister would be. So, not as me but as an old woman, I saw that Anna now has a protection rune where the old scratch existed. That can only come from one entity: the Mother Goddess," Laurie stated. Daniel looked confused and tried to follow, but he felt lost now. She could tell by his facial expressions.

"Oh, it gets better. Although your mother is a high priestess, she really doesn't have any powers. Yet she's getting them from somewhere," Laurie said.

"Are you saying that my mother is hiding the altar?" Daniel asked sternly.

"That's where I cannot see the connection. I can say this. The shadow existed before the curse in Beith, and it is as though someone here has taken over. Like now, they are allowing the shadow to be here, but they don't know it. Or they do and are just not saying anything," Laurie explained.

"What does my sister have to do with this, then? Is Sabrina affected as well?" Daniel asked concernedly.

"I think Sabrina is safe since she is not here. She's with your auntie, right?" Laurie asked.

"That's right," Daniel replied.

"Anna, since the shadow physically touched her, may have a connection with it but may not realize it. Have you noticed any odd behavior with her?" Laurie asked.

"No, not that I have seen. But before you ask me anything else, you can transform into another human? I think I'm still stuck on that," Daniel said as he rubbed his head. His eyes were wide with amazement. Then he continued. "I didn't know Druids could do that! Now that is awesome!"

"You mean, you're totally not weirded out? You still want to be with me?" Laurie asked, surprised.

"Oh, don't get me wrong, I'm weirded out! But I absolutely still want to be with you! Are you kidding me?" Daniel stated enthusiastically. Daniel could see the sigh of relief and the weight dropping off her shoulders. He continued. "You have been open and honest with me, and that's more than I can say for some of my mates. I have questions, though. Is my family in danger, or are we just being protected? Is what you told me a clue to finding the altar? What would make the shadow stay in Beith?" Daniel asked calmly. He was sincere, but his mind was buzzing like a swarm of bees. Anything was possible. If anyone were to express this outside of Beith, they probably would have been locked up for sure.

"Again, that part I don't know. I wish I could tell you for sure. I hope what I discovered is getting closer to finding the altar. I believe it's hidden, but by what or whom is the mystery. Which ties into why the shadow is here in the first place. It had to have made a pact with someone," Laurie explained.

"What does the shadow want?" Daniel asked intently.

"Souls, I presume. It really doesn't have a purpose other than to destroy us for something sinister. That is just a guess, by the way," Laurie explained.

"How did it come to be? The shadow," Daniel asked.

"Another good question. Someone conjured the shadow. Maybe that person was a new Druid experimenting with the dark book or someone that knew exactly what they were doing and wanted to gain power by causing chaos," Laurie expressed.

"The dark book?" Daniel tilted his head a little, displaying a discerning look.

"Druids are very much for the love of nature, the elements, and the seasons. We understand that in order to have harmony, there needs to be a balance between congruence and unrest. Some are not patient. They were given a gift to provide harmony within a grove and yet wanted excessive power or a connection with the earth. There lies the unrest," Laurie explained as her eyes welled with tears.

Daniel grabbed her hands and gave her a slight smile. He kissed the insides of her hands and pulled her closer to hold him.

"Sounds like people take advantage of this gift. Is there a type of Druid that can help other Druids steer away from the 'unrest'? Or help with your theories?" Daniel asked while placing soft kisses on the top of her head.

"I've never met one, but if there was a mix of a witch and Druid, maybe," Laurie replied.

"Aren't witches bad?" Daniel asked.

"Ah, no, not necessarily. There are white and dark witches. White witches are healers and guardians. Dark witches, well, they're just evil bitches." Laurie laughed.

While holding Laurie, Daniel looked at his watch.

"Shit! Time for you to get to class already!"

"Thank you for everything! You're the best!" Laurie exclaimed.

They stood up and kissed each other. Laurie grabbed her food and drink and headed to class. Daniel stayed by the tree, trying to grasp what he had heard. Luckily, Jeremy and Christian broke his thoughts.

"Hey, you two all right, mate?" Jeremy asked.

"Oh yeah. We are definitely good. Laurie is just a bit tired of this shadow stuff and wanted to chat is all," Daniel replied. There was no way he would tell them what Laurie had said. It was still too much for him to comprehend, and he probably needed another day to process it.

"Geez, look at him. Never seen one that big before," Christian said, pointing up to one of the tree's top branches where a raven stood. The raven cawed and then flew away.

"Did you get the ravenMcDonald's too?" Daniel tried to laugh it off, but he remembered what Laurie had said about the ravens.

"You ready for the science test?" Jeremy asked.

"As ready as I'll ever be," Daniel replied.

Daniel got home from school and pondered deeply what Laurie had said. It was odd that no one was home, as normally Mum was dashing about making supper. He decided to call his auntie Irene in Edinburgh to see if she knew anything.

"Hi, Auntie. How are you?" Daniel said with a smile. "Can I say hi to Sabrina?" he asked.

"Hello, laddie. Where's that crazy sister of mine? Doing 'this and that,' I suppose," Irene said jokingly.

"Not sure, really," Daniel replied, shrugging his shoulders.

"Here's your sister," Irene said.

A bright, smiling twelve-year-old young girl showed on the monitor. She was starting to wear a little mascara on her lashes around her crystal-blue eyes. She had thick eyebrows and natural platinum-blond hair with a hint of auburn. She was slender and always wore her favorite color, purple.

"Hey, Daniel! It's good to see you! When are you comin' to Auntie's house?" Sabrina asked excitedly.

"Soon, hopefully soon. Things are getting weird around here. I know you don't want to hear it but let's just say my mates, partner, and others are finding clues about the shadow. I'm glad you are there where it's safe," Daniel stated. He gave a slight smile her way.

"Yeah, me too. Like, I don't mind hearing about it as long as that thing doesn't come for me. And, of course, I don't want it to hurt you, Anna, or Mum, but you know. Dad," Sabrina said as she looked down to the ground, trying to hold back the tears.

"I'm sorry. I shouldn't have said anything. I just thought you would kind of want to know. So, tell me about school. What are you into?" Daniel asked, trying to change the subject.

"No worries. Nothing to be sorry for, and I appreciate it. Just stay safe," Sabrina said. Then her demeanor changed as she talked about school. "Oh, I'm a junior squad cheerleader. Because I'm the lightest, I get to be flipped in the air," she said excitedly.

"Oh, geez. Don't tell Mum that. She will worry all day and night thinking you'll break your neck," Daniel said. Then there was a long pause.

"Hey!" Daniel stated.

"Hey, what, you goof?" Sabrina replied, smiling.

"Make sure you ring Mum, OK? She misses you," Daniel said softly but sternly, looking at her like she'd better do it.

"OK, OK. Just busy is all," Sabrina explained.

"Not busy enough for family, though. Find the time," Daniel demanded but in a brotherly way.

"OK, I get it. Hush it already!" Sabrina laughed.

"You hush!" Daniel laughed right back at her. "OK, let me talk to Auntie, please. Love you," Daniel said. His eyes drooped as he realised how much he missed his little sister. Daniel was seventeen, graduating from secondary school. He wasn't sure about anything at the moment other than that he loved Laurie, something weird was going on with his family, and apparently, people were getting closer to finding the altar. He had to gain clarity, and hopefully, his auntie could help. Soon, a thin woman with gray hair and reading glasses appeared.

"Well, you absolutely made her day," Auntie Irene said.

"Has she not been OK? What is she not telling me?" Daniel asked, concerned.

"Oh, she's fine, laddie, but there is a difference between living here in Edinburgh versus living in a small town. It took her a little bit, but she is finally making strides at school. Making new friends, that sort of thing. Nothing to be too concerned about," Irene said, assuring him.

"Well, that's good," Daniel said.

"OK, lad, spill it!" Irene said. Daniel took a deep breath.

"What do you know about the altar, the shadow, and the mess going on here?" Daniel said bluntly. "I was told today that somehow our family is involved." Daniel was frantic at this point and didn't know where to turn.

"Oh my. I knew this conversation would be brought up sooner than later. My sister, your mother, your grandmother, and your grandmother's sister were all in that Druid stuff. I wasn't into that. You know me; God is number one," Irene said proudly.

"Yeah, I know. We're a mixed bag here. Or we were anyway. I don't know what we do or believe in anymore," Daniel said.

"I believe it was my aunt who got into some dark magic of some sort, but I don't think that has anything to do with the shadow there," Irene said.

Daniel felt he wasn't getting much help, but then he remembered what Laurie said to him earlier. Then he yelled out, "Dark book!"

"Goodness! What are you going on about?" Irene was startled. She could see Daniel's eyes as though he had just gotten a clue to help solve part of a mystery.

"My partner said that the shadow might have been conjured by dark magic from the dark book," Daniel said, hoping to get answers.

Irene knew what he was talking about but didn't want to give further details to protect him. That was one book no one should venture to read. It could cause more harm than good to the innocent.

"I take it she's a Druid, then. Has she dabbled with dark magic?" Irene asked probingly.

"Gee, Auntie, I don't know. I sure hope not!" Daniel felt despair in the pit of his stomach. He then felt flushed.

"I only ask because of how conversant she is with this 'dark book of dark magic.' Wouldn't you agree?" Irene asked.

"I'll have to talk with her again about it," Daniel said, feeling deflated, not getting the information he needed.

"I have to get going, love, but you take care of yourself. Take care of Anna and your mum. You are the man of the house," Irene said.

"Yes, ma'am. Thank you for everything, though. I'll come by after the jubilee," Daniel said. He knew his auntie was going to ask anyway.

"Oh, good. It will be wonderful having you here, love. Take care, Daniel. Love you," Irene said lovingly before the monitor went blank.

Daniel's mind was now going a mile a minute. What if Laurie tried to tell him that she was hiding the altar? She had even said that her transformation powers were deteriorating. He wondered if she knew more than what she had told him.

He heard the garage door opening. Daniel thought to himself, *Oh boy, here they all come.*

As Agnes, Anna, William, and Nancy walked in, they all looked like they had been emotionally dragged through the mud.

"What the hell happened to you guys?" Daniel exclaimed.

"Not now, lad. It was a rough afternoon," Agnes said lethargically, waving her hand gently, indicating they shouldn't bother her.

"Mum, I know you had a bad afternoon, but I need to talk to you about something. It's vital," Daniel said anxiously.

"If it has to do with the shadow or anything like that, then not now, love," Agnes said.

Nancy headed home, Anna went upstairs to shower, and William stayed downstairs to wait on Anna.

Daniel would have to get his mother's attention sooner rather than later and also find a way to approach Laurie on what she *really* knew about the shadow.

Chapter 7

Q AND A

After a long day with Agnes, Nancy went home to get a decent night's sleep. She was proper exhausted from the night before, yet Nancy felt stirred. Something wasn't sitting right with her.

"I know that look. What is ye thinking about, love?" John asked. A slender yet built man, John worked out even at the age of forty-nine. He had brown hair that was trimmed business-style and warm blue eyes that would calm Nancy's soul whenever she got upset. Those eyes she needed now, and he knew it.

"Agnes and I have been mates and neighbors for over ten years," Nancy said.

"Close to two decades. Correct," John said.

"It seems that she's hiding something," Nancy stated.

John raised his eyebrow, now intrigued by his wife's theories. Somehow, she always ended up being right about things He then sat down next to her in his brown recliner, the one he'd been known to fall asleep in from time to time, watching the late news. While holding his cup of autumn-blend tea, he asked, "What are you saying?"

"I'm saying, every time I ask what she's been up to, she always responds, 'this and that.' It's funny at first, as though it's a joke, and I thought after she said that, she would actually tell me. Then Agnes would immediately change the subject with a slight smirk on her face. I just want to slap it off her and know what's going on!" Nancy said profoundly, then sighed, with her eyebrows downward.

"What do you suppose is going on?" John asked.

"I'm not sure. But it seems to do with the shadow covering Beith. As if she knows something about it. As if she's a part of it." She said the last part with her voice lowered. As she stared into the distance, Nancy said, "She told me today at lunch that she was voted as high priestess by the grove but not by the spirits. Or however that works."

"Sweetheart, you know her daughter, Anna, witnessed her father taken by that shadow thing. Agnes is probably trying to keep calm and keep her family intact. The family lost their father, Agnes her husband. Maybe with her witchy ways she's trying to find how to destroy this entity. I'm certain your best mate wouldn't betray you. Maybe her eldritch ways are difficult to explain," John said with a grin. He was trying to bring a positive perspective to the situation but seemed to be failing. He, too, couldn't imagine Agnes being part of the shadow madness. Nancy rolled her eyes and said, "She's a Druid priestess, and yes, their beliefs, teachings, and ceremonies are *different*, but her intentions are to protect the grove, which is also important to her. You're probably right, love. It's just so preternatural for her to keep a secret. Especially from me!"

"She's probably found something which could be dangerous and wants to protect you. Let's say that is the case. Are you willing to get involved in that type of danger?" John looked at her and pointed in a way to suggest she needed to think about it unfeigned.

"Hmm, a Druid priestess can't figure out what took her husband, let alone this town. I still think something is afoot!" Nancy stated with disdain.

John walked over to her, put down his tea, and held her hand with both of his. As he looked at her with compassion, he said, "Darlin', whenever you get like this, I know you won't stop until you know the truth. We know that no matter what action is taken against the dark shadow, there will be danger. It's inevitable, of course. Don't take unnecessary risks, but I support you in whatever you decide. Talk to Agnes."

"Are you sure?" Nancy asked.

"Well, do I really have a choice in the matter? You won't rest until your nosy intuitions are proved right or wrong," John said sarcastically.

"Gee, thanks, love. Being cheeky, are we?" Nancy said, returning the sarcasm.

John finished his tea, kissed Nancy on the forehead, and got ready for bed. Nancy continued to sit in the chair, contemplating how to approach Agnes. A few moments later, she went to bed, wondering what she should do, uncertain of the dangers that lay ahead. What if the shadow came for

John? Or James? Yet many lives had been taken as though a sacrifice was needed. Then it dawned on her. *Wait! What if that was it? Agnes knew what the shadow wanted!* Nancy continued to toss and turn in bed, trying to figure out what to do. Then, with determination suffusing her face, she decided to approach Agnes tomorrow and demand answers!

At the first break of dawn, Nancy's alarm went off at 7:00. Feeling confident about her decision, she started getting ready for the day and noticed John was in the shower. With a slight grin and naughty thoughts stirring, she took off her rose-colored nightgown and stepped into the shower with him. Without saying a word, she took the loofah and lathered it with soap. She washed his back, then down his legs. She gently washed his chest—she loved running her fingers through his chest hair. Nancy started to tease him, touching him. John passionately kissed her and grabbed her waist. He moved to kissing her large breasts and then moved between her legs. Her moaning aroused him more, and they continued until they both climaxed. John kissed her, slowly moving up, sucking the droplets on her skin until they were face-to-face. They kissed each other as though they were sixteen again. John washed Nancy and continued to be playful.

"I love you, but I have to get going for Anna's appointment. Now that dessert is out of the way, I'll go make breakfast," Nancy said quietly and giggled.

John slapped her butt as she got out of the shower. Nancy got dressed: jeans, a rust-colored sweater, and brown boots. With that extra energy boost, she was ready to approach Agnes. Yet it would be tricky, considering today was Anna's appointment and the focus should be on Anna. Getting Agnes's focus would be a bit difficult. In the meantime, Nancy made sure John had a huge breakfast and coffee before work.

"Hello, my beautiful wife!" John gleefully stated as he entered the kitchen. He continued. "Everything looks wonderful, thank you!" He gave Nancy a long kiss and another swat on the butt.

Nancy smiled and said, "You're welcome."

"So, have you come up with a strategy on how you're going to address your concerns to Agnes?" John asked, then took a sip of his coffee.

"It will be challenging today because the focus is on Anna. I'm unsure how or when I'll approach the topic, but it must be sooner than later," Nancy said before letting out a deep breath.

"Well, I should be home by four. I have a surprise for you," John said with a smile while putting on his coat.

"What's the surprise?" Nancy asked excitedly.

"Hmm, just don't make any plans with Agnes this weekend," John said, grabbing his coffee.

"OK, love," Nancy said as she bit her bottom lip. They kissed, and John headed out the door. She cleaned up and headed over to Agnes's house.

Nancy got to Agnes's house and rang the door. The monitor in the kitchen alerted Agnes that someone was there.

"Anna, go see who's at the door, love," Agnes said.

"It's Ms. Nancy," Anna replied. Anna let her in, and of course Nancy was entertained by Agnes zipping about the house completing last-minute chores.

"How are you, Ms. Nancy?" Anna asked with a smile. "As you can see, Mum is buzzing about the kitchen."

"So I see. Nothing new then," Nancy said, laughing.

"I heard that!" Agnes yelled from another room.

"Oh, I'm sure you did," Nancy said sarcastically.

"OK, you two, let's get going. The appointment is at nine a.m. sharp," Anna said as she picked up her purse and headed out the door.

"Well, I guess little missy here just told us!" Agnes said. Both Agnes and Nancy laughed.

Anna got into the back seat and put in her earbuds. She knew what this appointment was for, so the techno sounds of DJ Rambler soothed her. Nancy sat up front with Agnes and waited before asking Agnes anything. It was roughly a forty-five-minute drive to the east part of Glasgow, so there had to be a good time to talk. Not exactly the best part of the city, but that was where Dr. Stone's office was located. Anna stared out the window at the trees with their fall colors on display. Anna's smile quickly reverted to that of concern. Then a text popped up from William.

"Just thinking about you. Hope things go well today." It ended with a heart and a kiss emoji. Anna smiled and texted back.

"Thank you, sweetheart. I'll let you know what happens."

"OK, I'll be here!" William responded.

Anna smiled, took a deep breath, and returned to her music.

"You OK, Anna?" Agnes asked, looking at Anna from her rearview mirror.

"I'm good, Mum. Just listening to music," Anna replied, then showed a half smile her mum could see from the mirror.

"OK, love," Agnes replied.

About fifteen minutes went by, and Agnes was worried about the appointment and also quite confused about why Nancy wasn't too chatty.

"Nancy, what is going on with you? What do you want to talk to me about?" Agnes asked while trying to concentrate on the road. Looking ahead, she noticed the traffic starting to slow down.

"Dè tha an ifrinn a 'dol?" Agnes asked out loud, not directing it to anyone.

Nancy knew Agnes was troubled when she started speaking Scottish Gaelic. She wished she understood, but she got the gist based on Agnes's tone of voice. The dead language was now taught only through old videos found from 2024, and that was if there was a genuine interest. It was scarce to see the language passed down to future generations.

"Well, it's a good thing we left when we did. I heard they are emplacing radar and boundary transmitters for the hover vehicles," Nancy said

"Clearly not soon enough. We might be late!" Agnes replied frantically.

"Calm down. We can exit up here at the M77, then to the A726, turn left on M74, then north on M8 back into Glasgow," Nancy said.

"Goodness, Nancy. Just tell me ahead of time where I'm to turn," Agnes said.

"OK." Nancy laughed.

As they entered Glasgow, Anna was amazed by the tall glass buildings. It had been so long since Agnes and Nancy had been there that it still felt like the first time. People walked about as though they had no cares in the world.

"Oh my, I remember when I was a wee one and came through here. It looked all run-down. Glass and brick buildings that looked like they were built in the late nineteenth century," Agnes said as she looked around. Now the streets were wider, with more trees and brightly colored flowers at every corner, and buildings upgraded to resemble towers, then square buildings."

"Oh wow! Anna, look at that!" Nancy announced.

While stopped at the light, Anna looked out the window and noticed a car-show exhibit along a blocked-off road. People were showing off their new cars. One didn't have tires but seemed to be hovering above the ground. Anna looked with amazement. The shadow was the only thing she had ever seen hover. Many cars were lined up with their hoods up, clearly showing off their engines.

"That's really cool. I'm sure William would have liked to be here to see that," Anna replied. She took some photos to share with William.

They approached another area close to the river. Where four buildings used to be in a row on each side, now there was a smooth pebble walkway to the left and right of the stoplight. The eateries near the river had four rows of tables with umbrellas. To the right side of the traffic light were vendors selling their goods. There was a band playing music in the background. Anna noticed that many of the pebbles made a design. Some were flowers, one a unicorn, one a tree with faeries flying, and another an area with a castle. Anna photographed everything she saw. It was as though they were traveling to a distant land. So many improvements had been made since King Andrew II became king.

"You think we could have something like this in Beith someday?" Anna asked.

"I don't know, but this certainly would be nice," Nancy replied.

"Where is this road? Did I miss my turn? Too busy looking at all this got me turned around," Agnes said.

"Next light, turn left," Nancy replied.

"Oh, thank you, love," Agnes said, sighing with relief.

As they arrived, they looked upon the two-story rectangular tan building surrounded by a red iron fence. Perfectly trimmed bushes, including rose bushes of reds, pinks, and yellows, accented the fence line. Anna immediately felt like she had been tricked into going to a mental ward rather than a psychology appointment. There were twelve identical windows on the top and bottom of the building and a red entry door to match the security gate. Outside the neatly trimmed landscape, it didn't seem very welcoming.

As they approached the front desk, they were scornfully greeted by a short young woman.

"Hello, sign in the book, and you'll be called when they're ready to see ye," the lady said. She stood about 160 centimeters and had long brown hair with curls at the end and hazel eyes. She was so thin Agnes wanted to get her a double cheeseburger. Agnes saw how Anna was scared and tried to ease her mind. Anna overheard the woman and was in shock.

"Anna, we are in the big city, and people are different here. They are not as personable because they don't know us. Everything will be OK," Agnes said as she hugged Anna.

Anna only wanted William to be by her side but didn't want to ring him over what she thought were petty feelings.

A few moments later, you could hear the clacking of high-heeled shoes coming down the echoing hallway. A slender woman wearing a gray suit appeared with her blond hair in a bun.

"Anna Aird?" she asked with a smile. Anna grinned.

"Dr. Stone will see you now, love. Right this way," she said.

As they started walking down the long corridor to Dr. Stone's office, the lady said, "Hello, Miss Aird. I understand you are from Beith."

"Yes," Anna replied sheepishly.

"We still can't believe the stories of the dark shadow that looms over your town," the receptionist said.

"I guess that's why I'm here," Anna said quietly.

"Well, do not fear, lass. Dr. Stone is amazing, and I'm sure he will be able to assist in whatever troubles you have," the receptionist said lovingly.

"Let's hope," Anna replied.

They reached the tall solid-wood door. The receptionist opened it, and at first glance, it looked as though they had entered a library. Books were stacked almost as tall as the ceiling. To the left was an old light-wood rectangular table with two chairs, possibly Dr. Stone's break and reading area. Straight ahead as you walked in was his main desk, a very thick solid-oak desk, roughly two and a half meters wide. Psychology books on his right, pictures of his family in the center, and an award for the 2075 Psychologist of the Year with other personal items surrounding it. Directly behind him was one of the tall windows.

"Dr. Stone. This is Anna Aird of Beith," the receptionist introduced gleefully.

"Thank you," Dr. Stone said.

The receptionist smiled at Anna and walked out the door. Dr. Stone noticed Anna squinting from the window and lowered the blinds.

"Is that better?" Dr. Stone asked with a slight smile.

"Yes, thank you, sir," Anna replied.

"Please, make yourself comfortable," Dr. Stone said.

Anna looked at the long chaise furnished with pillows and a blanket. There was a small table with fresh roses in a vase next to the chaise. Anna removed her shoes, leaned against the pillows, and put the blanket over her. She noticed the little refrigerator next to his desk, and her eyes widened when she saw the Irn-Bru cans.

"Miss Aird, may I offer you a beverage? I can have the receptionist get you some tea or coffee. Or perhaps you would like an Irn-Bru?" Dr. Stone asked.

"An Irn-Bru, please!" Anna said excitedly.

"Irn-Bru for the young lady," Dr. Stone said as he handed her the can. It was nice and cold, and she knew it would taste perfect.

"As the receptionist said, I am Dr. Stone. I have been a psychologist for twenty-two years now. I must admit, my normal patients are adults, but lately, I have been interested in Beith's activities. It has been such a phenomenon, the missing altar. So when the receptionist received your mother's call, I made an exception. I want you to know that you are safe here. I will sit at my desk, you at the chaise or the other table. Whatever makes you comfortable. If you don't feel like talking, that is also understandable. I am here to listen and analyze in hopes of making you have less stress. How does that sound, Miss Aird?" Dr. Stone wanted to reassure Anna as much as possible. Trust was key, especially as an outsider, and he had never been to Beith before.

"That's fine," Anna said.

"Is it OK that I call you Anna? Or do you prefer Miss Aird for now?" Dr. Stone asked calmly.

"Anna is fine," she said quietly. The light-blue blanket covered her up to her eyes.

Dr. Stone started writing on his notepad.

"What are you writing? Do you think I'm crazy already?" Anna asked abruptly.

"Anna, no. Not at all. I am just going to ask some questions and am prepping questions at the moment and gathering my thoughts," Dr. Stone replied softly

"Oh, OK. Would you tell me if you thought I was crazy?" Anna asked.

"Anna, I don't think you are crazy at all. I think you, along with many others from Beith, have suffered much emotional trauma. I would like to get you back on track, so to speak, so you can better deal with your trauma. How does that sound?" Dr. Stone asked.

"Sounds good," Anna responded. She then sat up and drank some of her Irn-Bru. After some gulps, she rendered an enormous smile.

"I will let the receptionist know to stock up on Irn-Bru when you have your next appointment," Dr. Stone said with a slight smile.

"Thank you, sir. I mean, Dr. Stone," Anna said with appreciation.

Dr. Stone was stocky, not fat but not too skinny. He stood approximately 173 centimeters, with thick gray-and-brown hair that was mostly gray, bushy eyebrows, and sky-blue eyes. He wore a college ring on his right hand with a rectangular amethyst in the center. He wore a navy-blue suit with a yellow-and-navy-blue tie.

"So, I'm going to ask some questions just to get an idea of what might be happening. Is there anything you wish to ask me before I begin?" Dr. Stone asked.

"No," Anna replied quietly.

"Very well then. Anna, how old are you?"

"Fifteen," Anna replied.

"Do you take any drugs or drink alcohol?" Dr. Stone asked.

"No," Anna replied softly.

"How long have you been living in Beith?" he asked.

"All my life," she replied.

"When did you start to notice the shadow in Beith?" he asked.

"A few years ago, when my friend Brandon had his sister taken away," she responded.

"Taken away by a person or by the shadow?" he asked.

"By the shadow," she replied.

"How did that affect you?" he asked.

"I felt bad for him. I was sad too. Like, his losing a sister made me think about how devastated I would be if I lost Sabrina or Daniel," Anna stated.

"Are Sabrina and Daniel your sister and brother?" he asked.

"Yes," she replied.

"Has the shadow affected you personally?" he asked.

"Yes. The shadow took my father, and I don't think my mum has fully forgiven me," Anna said as she started to cry a wee bit. Tears rolled down past her chin.

"Forgiven you? Could you please expound on that?" he asked.

"It was night, and I heard something outside. But when I opened the door, my father ran towards me to close it. It was too late. The shadow grabbed him and shot up, then immediately went to the ground. I don't want to talk about that anymore." Anna felt so guilty, and now she thought this doctor was going to tell her she was crazy.

"Anna. You have nothing to feel guilty about," he said. Anna looked at him intently as that was exactly what she needed to hear, but she would have loved to hear it from her mum.

"Thank you. But you believe that. My mum, on the other hand, does not," Anna retorted.

"Has she said that?" he asked.

"No, but like, I know she loves me, but I don't think she has forgiven me for Father being gone," Anna explained.

"Ah, I see. Do you need to take a break?" he asked.

"No, but may I please have another Irn-Bru?" Anna asked with a smile.

"Absolutely, lass. You can have as many as you want," he replied with enthusiasm. He reached into the mini refrigerator and pulled out another Irn-Bru, then opened the can and placed it next to her. He sat back down in his posh leather chair and continued.

"Have you seen things out of the ordinary? Like other than shadows, people that are there one minute and not there the next," he asked.

"I was in the woods, trying to pick gems, but this crone was washing my father's bloody shirt. I followed her to this shack, but when I opened the door, she was gone, and it was empty inside. The chimney was still spewing white smoke. When I returned to where I usually pick up gems, the washboard was gone, and she was gone," Anna explained.

"Was that a dream you had?" he asked. Dr. Stone had to cover all bases because any facial expression could cause the questioning to stop. Just with this conversation, he knew what Anna was facing. From all the patients he had seen from Beith, he knew something ominous was happening.

"Don't freak out, but it was reality," Anna said with a hint of sarcasm.

"Have you seen anything else?" he asked.

"Well, I had a nightmare the other day after I rushed home from the old-crone incident. I took a nap, and there was this person calling for the shadow next to the altar. It was a demon princess and the shadow talking. Before I woke up, the shadow said he was coming for me, and his face, or basically a dark mass, came to me. As though he was right there!" Anna exclaimed and then added, "Then what was once a scar is now a rune and was glowing when I woke up. Is it OK if I show you my rune?"

"Absolutely!" Dr. Stone responded eagerly.

Anna rolled up her sleeve and showed him the markings on her arm.

"Where did this come from? I don't think I have seen anything like this before. Why do you call it a rune, may I ask?" he inquired.

"Well, not sure where it came from, and when I did some research, it is more like a protection rune," Anna replied.

"May I please take a picture so I may do some follow-on research?" he asked.

Dr. Stone pulled out his mobile and snapped a picture of her arm and then inquired, "Who else knows about these markings?"

"Pretty much everyone now. We just spent a few hours down by the loch yesterday showing my mum, Ms. Nancy, and William where the crone was," Anna replied.

"I take it Ms. Nancy and William are friends?" he asked.

"Yes. Ms. Nancy is my mum's mate, and William is my boyfriend," Anna replied.

"Ah, I see. Does William treat you well?" he asked like a concerned parent.

"Oh, absolutely! If it weren't for him, I probably wouldn't be able to face all this alone," Anna said. When she talked about William, her face lit up.

"Young love. Those days were long ago for me," he said with a quick laugh. "Anna, although you are fifteen, you are still protected under the privacy act. If you don't want me to discuss anything with your mother, I won't," he assured her.

"Just don't tell her I'm crazy." Anna looked at him nervously.

"Anna, you don't have to worry about that," he said with a smile. He picked up the receiver and talked to the receptionist.

"Please escort Anna to the waiting area. I'm ready to talk with Mrs. Aird now," Dr. Stone stated.

"Right away, doctor," the receptionist responded.

A few moments later, the receptionist opened the door and smiled at Anna.

"Right this way, love." The receptionist motioned toward the hallway.

Dr. Stone picked up the phone, dialed a number, and stated, "It's true; she is the one we have been looking for." He hung up the phone and displayed a sinister grin. He pondered a bit because he felt absolutely sorry for Anna's pain, mental and physical. He quickly changed his grin back to an expression of a professional psychologist prepared to talk with Anna's mother to discuss his findings. The receptionist brought Agnes to Dr. Stone's office.

"Ah, Mrs. Aird. Please have a seat," he said as he un-buttoned a button from his suit jacket. "Can I offer you something to drink?" he asked with a slight smile.

"No, no, thank you," Agnes said quickly. She wanted to get down to the point and skip the small talk. Her eyes were wide open, and she desperately wanted his view even though she knew exactly what was happening.

"So, tell me directly what's goin' on with Anna, please," she said with a bit of sternness.

Dr. Stone sat down in his brown leather chair and looked at Agnes for a few seconds.

"Ma'am…," Dr. Stone began.

"Please, call me Agnes," she interrupted.

"Well, Agnes, what I must tell you requires a bit of explanation. But first, Anna is under the patient-doctor protection, which basically protects the client's confiden-tiality. However, she did agree to allow me to acknowl-edge what I presume is her current situation. First of all, I wanted to thank you for bringing Anna to me. Like I told Anna, I have been quite intrigued about Beith and the paranormal activity there. Anna is not my first patient from Beith. People from there tend to think they are go-ing crazy, turning schizophrenic. However, the activity surrounding Beith is a catalyst to second- and third-order effects that invoke on the unconscious mind," Dr. Stone stated.

"What exactly are you saying?" Agnes asked sharply.

"I am saying, Mrs. Aird, your daughter has a severe case of PTSD—post-traumatic stress disorder—and a bit of psychosis. She is a perfectly normal young lady. She has a supportive family and partner, but she feels you have not forgiven her for when the shadow took her father. This is not to say anything is your fault; it is to say some communication would help. Express your feelings on the matter," Dr. Stone said expressively.

"To tell ye the truth, I have been upset about it but not at her. There aren't enough bolt locks on that door to keep her curious mind at bay. I will chat with her for sure," Agnes said, her eyes filling up with tears. Dr. Stone handed her a tissue, then sat at the edge of his desk.

"Well, the sooner, the better. Plus, there is another matter. Any other psychologist would likely describe Anna as having residual schizophrenia. It seems Anna is being used somehow by this entity, the shadow. I don't understand it yet, but I would like to do something called cognitive behavioral therapy. I would like to see if some of the root issues of her anxiety enhance the shadow's activity."

"Wouldn't that be dangerous?" Agnes exclaimed.

"Not necessarily, but if she can conquer some of the forces working against her, this entity may not use her. It sounds all bizarre, but I would need more time to pinpoint it effectively," he stated. He saw that Agnes was still trying to process what she had just heard.

"Is there something you would like to add that might help?" he asked. He felt as though she was hiding something.

"No, no. Nothing. I'm just trying to understand all this," Agnes said, staring at the corner of the room.

"Agnes." He tried to get her attention.

"Yes, sorry." Agnes became aware again.

"Let's get you back to the front and schedule another appointment in two weeks," he said as he stood up and started walking to the door.

"Do you have any questions for me?" he asked.

"She doesn't require medication, does she?" Agnes asked.

"No," he responded with a smile.

"Thank you again, Dr. Stone. Very much appreciatin' ye," Agnes responded with a feeling of hope, and she displayed a slight smile.

They got to the car, and Agnes stood at the driver's side. She faced Anna and gave her a look of adoration.

"Anna, please accept my apology for not talkin' with ye about your father. You did nothing wrong, and there is nothing to forgive." Agnes and Anna held each other. Agnes could feel the heartache releasing from her body.

"Thank you, Mum." Anna smiled. They got into the car and headed home.

Chapter 8

KNOWLEDGE IS EVERYTHING

Upon the hallowed grounds of Daegal, the Druids met again to converse about dealing with the current state of affairs, being *the Shadows* that cover Beith. An initiation was happening. Typically, the initiation would be under a new moon, either during the day or at night. Now the grove waited for the spirit's decision: either accept the initiation by a sacred flame or deny by freezing the water in the chalice.

"Who brings in the initiate?" Agnes asked profoundly.

"I do," replied Judy. Judy then brought the initiate forward and presented her to the high priestess.

"What makes this lass worthy of joining the order?" Agnes asked.

"High Priestess, the initiate was given the gift of sight. Her mother gave her the gift when she passed. The initiate has seen firsthand the ways of the shadows. Her insights and visions have proved true and are instrumental to our cause. She serves only the Goddess and is willing to expand her knowledge and training through our grove," Judy said with determination.

Agnes raised the chalice and the scepter and looked toward the sky. "Great Goddess Druantia, hear our plea. We ask for your guidance and blessing upon our grove and seek your will upon this initiate."

After she said these words, the air remained still. The water did not freeze yet moved gently within the chalice. The pit filled with wood remained dry. The other Druids were becoming restless as no answer appeared, as though the Goddess had forgotten about them. Agnes realised the tension among them.

"We must remain patient. We wait on our Lady Goddess to assess her decision because she is perfect in her ways," Agnes said calmly and softly. The Druids closed their eyes and waited. Then flames of heavy fire lit the pit, and a massive sigh of relief came from them. There was cheering and constant congratulations!

"Sister Latrice, welcome to our grove. The Goddess finds favor with you and has allowed you to join our sister and brotherhood. I will speak with you soon to discuss your *gifts*. I'm quite intrigued. For now, we have matters to discuss. Again, welcome," Agnes said gently and with a smile.

Latrice gave a slight nod and said, "Thank you, High Priestess." She smiled and sat next to Judy.

"Sisters, brothers. It is time to have this meeting come to order. We must discuss the recent activities."

Agnes was interrupted by Jacquelyn. "I'm sick of discussing and not doing!" she yelled.

"Yield your tongue! You know we have to prepare before the festival," Agnes stated firmly.

The Druids looked at each other but didn't want to be ousted by the high priestess. Latrice slowly stood and meekly said, "If I may, High Priestess, with your permission and the sisters' and brothers' permission, call upon the spirits to uncover what's hidden."

There was some chatter among the other Druids, and all agreed it sounded like a great idea.

"We will do no such thing at this time!" Agnes said, standing unerring.

"Why not?" Brandon asked angrily. "It's the best idea we had since the shadow came to Beith!"

The other Druids agreed and looked at Agnes as though she was guilty of a crime. Agnes had to think quickly.

"Sisters and brothers, we must remember the rules of the Goddess. We are not to perform rituals or call upon the spirits unless granted by fire," Agnes said.

"Easy. Just ask the spirits!" Sebastian said plainly.

"Unless you're afraid to ask and currently hiding something from us," Kristine said sarcastically.

"Again, sisters and brothers, being demanding of the spirits can cause us to lose our relationship with them, and then where would we be? This is why during these uncertainties, I was granted high priestess. We must not take advantage of the spirits," Agnes said. She took a subtle deep breath, hoping that would calm them.

"Sometimes being a Druid is a waste of time. Our connection with the spirits is on their terms and never ours. Our time has been dire, and more of our families are becoming missing or dead. What are we to do?" Robert said with dread in his voice.

"We mustn't doubt our high priestess or the spirits. They have kept us alive this far. Plus, our time of victory must be at hand!" Judy said like a peppy cheerleader.

Latrice slowly sat back down with her arms folded. She wasn't feeling defeated, but all the information about the group seemed accurate, outside the high priestess. The high priestess seemed too unparalleled to the others. Not in the too-high-and-mighty sense, but she didn't fit with the rest of the group. Latrice really couldn't pinpoint it, but something was off for sure.

Latrice Beaumont stood 172 centimeters, with long whitish-blond hair, midtorso length. Her skin was pale white; the only color was the slight blush on her cheeks. Her eyes were oval-shaped and the shade of evening blue. She looked as though she came from elven roots: mysterious, mythical, yet powerful.

Latrice unfolded her arms and had a cheeky grin. She thought she would wait until later to conduct her spell.

Brandon noticed Latrice's facial expression and wondered what she might be thinking. He was determined to find out after the meeting. Brandon looked back at the high priestess and then at the others with his shifty eyes. Then he looked down to the ground, wondering whether or not the shadow would ever leave Beith. *Will the time of the conflict and young kings dim from our memories? Will Beith constantly live in fear?* Brandon became frustrated, picked up some rocks, and threw them back onto the ground. Shaking his head, he sighed, then looked back to the high priestess.

"Sisters and brothers, we thank the Goddess for our time together, and let us go in peace," Agnes said. All stood and started going their separate ways. Judy shifts her attention towards Latrice.

"You seem upset," Judy said with concern.

"I wouldn't necessarily say that, but there are things I don't quite understand," Latrice replied.

"Like what?" Judy asked. Her eyes widened as if to hear some grand news.

Latrice took a deep breath and exhaled quickly to show a sign of frustration.

"Well, can we go somewhere to talk? There are too many *ears*."

"Absolutely. You can trust me for sure. I think I know what you're going to say," Judy said with a reassuring slight smile.

As they started to walk off, Brandon grabbed Latrice's arm.

"Do you mind? How dare you!" Latrice snapped.

"Sorry…so sorry, it's just that I saw how you looked after the high priestess told you not to cast any spells," Brandon said calmly.

"Next time, don't grab my arm or I'll turn it into vines!" Latrice said sternly.

Judy and Brandon laughed, but Latrice remained firm. They stopped laughing and knew she meant business.

"Again, sorry, I just think we feel the same way. We are all frustrated with decades of shadows hovering over us. If you have an idea, I would love to hear it," Brandon said with sincerity.

"Most definitely! Even though I'm more of an ovate, I tend to revert to being a bard for the sake of the grove, especially when positivity seems lost. I, too, feel the darkness of the shadows and wonder at its hidden meaning," Judy confesses.

"You would be all daft not to feel such a way, Judy. I'm sure all are grateful for all you do for the grove," Brandon said with a smile as he hugged Judy.

"That's all fine and good, but right now, it's time to unearth the hidden altar," Latrice said as though she had just made a rallying cry for justice. "Come on, let's go to my house to discuss this further."

Both Judy and Brandon nodded their heads in compliance.

They reached the one-story brick home that had two large windows in the front and off-white shutters, a two-car garage, and a cared-for lawn with perfect edging. An off-white lamppost stood just a few feet from the main entrance, and a wooden swing hung from the edge of the porch.

"Wow! This house is nice!" Judy said.

"Yeah, most definitely!" Brandon exclaimed.

"Thanks!" Latrice said as they entered the house.

"Hey, Auntie. I brought mates over," Latrice said gleefully.

"Splendid! Hello, and welcome to our humble home. If it gets dark, you are welcome to stay here. Just notify your parents, of course," Catlin said gleefully.

Both Judy and Brandon replied, "Thank you, ma'am!"

"Oh, please, no formalities here. Call me Ms. Beaumont. Oh, heck, call me Catlin," she said joyfully. It was rare that Latrice would bring people to the house, so this was a real treat.

"Um, Ms. Catlin, I'm noticing some of the symbols around the house, and they look more Wiccan than Druid," Judy said.

"That's correct, lass. Latrice is a Druid, like her mother, and I'm Wiccan—a mage, to be precise. Latrice's father, James, was a warlock; therefore, Latrice has the best of both worlds," Catlin said proudly and smiled.

Judy snapped her head around and looked at Latrice. "That's it!"

"What's it?" Latrice asked.

"That's why the high priestess wouldn't let you call upon the spirits! She sensed you were both Druid and Wiccan. That's also why the Goddess took longer to make her decision. It makes sense now!" Judy exclaimed excitedly.

"Were you dedicated to the grove today, lass?" Catlin asked.

"Yes, Auntie," Latrice responded with disappointment. Her face partially dropped down, and she stared at the food on the countertop.

"You don't look so happy about it, love. Oh my! Where are my manners? Would any of you like some tea?" Catlin asked with slight embarrassment. She had an array of sandwiches, cookies, meats, beans, and chicken soup, enough to feed a small regiment. Catlin always cooked like that just in case people came over, especially if they had to stay late.

"Yes, ma'am," Brandon said, rubbing his hands together, excited to delve into the food. The girls chuckled at Brandon. Judy, being the polite soul that she always was, responded with, "Thank you. I would love to."

They each had some sandwiches and a large bowl of soup. Brandon took a bunch of cookies and put them on a plate beside his soup.

"OK, lass. What is on your mind?" Catlin asked Latrice. Catlin gently grabbed her hand from across the counter. She hated seeing her niece like this.

"I feel like the altar is hidden, and the high priestess has something to do with it," Latrice said plainly.

Judy and Brandon froze. Judy paused with the spoon in her mouth, and Brandon stopped crunching his cookie. Their eyes were as big as dinner plates, and it was as though time stood still. They were shocked that she had been daft enough to suggest such a thing. Latrice had just met her, she was dedicated to the grove, no less, and now she was assuming the high priestess was behind the shadow?

"Latrice, I think you're upset after feeling shafted by her. There's no way she's behind any of this! I would bet this delicious cookie on it," Brandon said jokingly.

"I'm serious! Why could we not ask the spirits? The Goddess? Other groves I was in would delight in evoking the spirits, giving us direction and peace. Today, the high priestess deterred us from doing so and gave bullshit as an excuse!" Latrice exclaimed angrily.

"The high priestess has never led us astray. If any-thing, she has brought us closer to the Goddess and nature and given us a better understanding of being a Druid. So much so I know an ovate is what I'm supposed to be," Judy snapped. However, at the same time, she was thinking, *How dare she speak against the high priestess!* She refrained from taking her thoughts too far and snapping again at her new friend.

"Judy, you all right? I never heard that tone from you before!" Brandon said. He felt like he needed to start walking on eggshells around Judy.

"I'm sorry. I—" Judy said before she was interrupted by Catlin.

"It's OK, lass. You are free to express yourself," Catlin said calmly.

"I'm not mad. It's just the way I feel," Latrice said, feeling defeated. Then she looked at Judy. "I'm sorry too," she said with a slight smile.

"Look, I don't think it's the high priestess, but there is definitely something afoot. Something is protecting the last altar. It makes no bloody sense!" Judy admits.

There was a bit of shock from Brandon. He had never heard Judy get so upset, but he also realized Judy was onto something.

"Auntie, you think maybe you could do a locator spell?" Latrice asked.

"I hate to disappoint you, lass, but I have nothing tan-gible binding to the altar itself. I could if someone has had contact with it," Catlin said.

"We have no way of knowing that unless we did a spell in front of the grove! UGH! Dang it! I wanted to try that but got shot down," Latrice said with frustration.

"Yeah, you were," Brandon said. Catlin, Judy, and Latrice all looked at Brandon angrily. Latrice rolled her eyes.

Judy looked outside and noticed the last light was about to fade.

"Ms. Catlin, is it OK that we stay the night?" Judy asked.

"Of course it is, lovies. Brandon, you can take the guest room, and the girls will be in Latrice's room," Catlin stated.

Judy and Brandon called their parents to let them know where they were and that they were safe. Of course, Brandon's father was not pleased but accepted it. Jack, Brandon's father, had always been strict about Brandon's whereabouts since the shadow took his little sister two years ago.

"All right then, but if anything feels wrong, let Ms. Catlin know immediately. And come straight home when the sun is high," Jack said with some shakiness in his voice.

"Of course, Dad," Brandon said to his dad respectfully while rolling his eyes.

After he got off the phone, he joined up with the ladies.

"Everything all right?" Latrice asked with concern.

"Yeah, my dad gets anxious when I'm not home since my sister died," Brandon said quietly.

"The shadows?" Latrice asked.

"Yeah," Brandon replied.

There was no complete explanation needed when the answer was the shadows.

"I'm so sorry, Brandon. Well, dinna fash, you are safe here. I say, maybe you three watch a movie in the living room. And, Brandon, you can have as many cookies as you like," Catlin said with a sly grin.

Brandon had a huge smile and grabbed the plate of cookies. The girls laughed, and then they all got comfortable in the living room.

"Which film do you guys wanna watch? An old film?" Latrice asked. "We have an old *Batman* film from 2022. Some hot guy is in that one," Latrice added.

"OH YES, PLEASE!" Judy exclaimed.

Brandon just rolled his eyes, but he liked action movies. He would tolerate being in the same room with them, just as long as he didn't have to hear all the girly stuff about some hot guy while watching.

"How many would love some super-buttered popcorn?" Catlin asked jovially.

"Cookies and popcorn? You spoil us, Ms. Catlin. Yes, please! And, um, can I come back next weekend too?" Brandon asked.

"What if I'm not here?" Latrice asked, looking at Brandon intently.

"That's OK. I'll just hang out with Ms. Catlin," Brandon said.

"WOW! Really?" Latrice bellowed.

Judy wasn't paying attention because she had noticed the hot guy on screen and tuned out everything that was going on around her.

"Latrice's friends are welcome anytime," Catlin said.

"Sweet!" Brandon said excitedly.

Catlin finished the popcorn and brought out two large bowls of perfectly made popcorn slathered in butter.

"Here ye go!" Catlin said with a smile. "I must complete some things as I'll be right back," Catlin added.

"Thanks, Ms. Catlin," Brandon said, sounding muffled since he had already stuffed his mouth with popcorn. Catlin got to her room and, before closing the door, made sure no one was coming down the hallway. She quietly closed the door, went to the back of the room, and made a phone call.

"Hello, Doctor. My niece has a theory but wanted to, of course, pass it by you first," Catlin said.

"What is the theory?" the doctor asked.

"She claims that the high priestess has something to do with the missing or hidden altar. Latrice wanted to call the spirits for help but was denied," Catlin explained.

"Yes, interesting. Your niece is very intuitive to her surroundings. Perhaps her focus should be directed on her daughter, Anna, rather than on the high priestess. I'm certain you can persuade your niece to befriend Anna," the doctor said. Then the doctor hung up.

Catlin felt scared. People, including her niece, were investigating why Beith was still in darkness. Usually, when Catlin spoke to the doctor, the doctor would reassure her that everything would be OK. Not this time. Catlin found it challenging to concentrate and was overwhelmed with anxiety. *Does the doctor believe people will find the hidden altar? Is Latrice in danger?* Catlin went to the water closet to splash some water on her face before re-joining the kids. She could change her demeanor like a chameleon and know something was wrong but, at the same time, act like all was well with the world. She steadily walked down the hallway and sat down on the chaise.

"What are we watching?" she asked.

"This is the old 2022 version of *Batman*. The guy who plays Batman is superhot! Oh, and by the way, Brandon ate all the popcorn. Do you have any more popcorn that we don't have to share with him?" Judy asked politely. They all laughed.

"Like, mate, how could you still be hungry?" Latrice asked.

"I don't know. Probably why my dad calls me the bot-tomless pit," Brandon replied.

"Of course! No worries at all, lovies. But Brandon, if you start eating everything, the next messages for my house will come out of your pocket!" Catlin laughed.

"Yes, ma'am," Brandon replied with a smile.

The girls devoured the popcorn. Even though Brandon would try and sneak some, Judy wouldn't allow it.

Later that evening, the girls were in Latrice's room, Ms. Catlin in hers, and Brandon in the guest bedroom just playing games on his mobile. Ms. Catlin heard the girls talking and decided to take this opportunity to speak with them about Anna. Catlin knocked on the door.

"Come in, Auntie," Latrice said. Catlin stood in the doorway with her finger and thumb on her chin in a thinking stance.

"Hello. I had an idea that maybe you two have already thought of, but maybe you can ask the high priestess's daughter if she knows anything. Do you know her name?"

"Her name is Anna. Ever since the shadow took her father, she has been homeschooled, I think," Judy said.

"How long ago was that?" Catlin asked.

"Um, about four months ago," Judy responded.

"That's horrible! It's still fresh in her mind, then. I cannae imagine what she's going through," Catlin said with concern. Then she tilted her head, and Latrice said, "I know that look. A bright idea is storming," Both girls looked at Catlin with anticipation.

"The jubilee is coming up. Ask her if she wants to hang out. Try to earn her trust and let her know that you both want the same thing: the shadow to be gone for good!" Catlin said exuberantly.

"Sounds like a good idea. Anna probably needs new friends right now anyway," Judy said.

"What are you all looking at?" Catlin asked curiously. Latrice had images of different shapes and symbols across her computer screen.

"We were just looking up protection runes," Latrice replied.

"Oh, I see. Are you possibly thinking one of these runes may be protecting the altar?" Catlin asked.

"Precisely!" Latrice responded. Then she continued. "Like, look at this one. It protects the person from the people around them. And this one, with all these circles and paisley shapes, protects against demons."

Latrice was a bit excited, feeling she had stumbled onto something.

"Maybe the next time you are at the grove, see if you can find such symbols," Catlin suggested.

"Good idea, but right now, we need to talk to Anna. Hopefully, she'll be at school Monday. Then next Saturday is the jubilee. Should be enough time," Latrice noted.

"I'll introduce you to her." Judy smiled.

"You would have a school assembly to introduce me to everyone if it were allowed." Latrice and Judy laughed.

"Facts!" Judy responded.

Daniel and Anna showed up at school. Anna watched as Christian and Jeremy gave Daniel the standard guy handshake.

Daniel looked at Anna and saw her uncertainty about showing up today. She would rather pick gems from the quarry than be at school; however, it was time to get back to normal. Then Judy walked up and was already expressing her bubbly personality, anxiously waiting to talk with Anna.

"Hi, Anna. Do you remember me? I'm Judy."

"Hi. Um, I think you are in my English class," Anna said hesitantly.

"Go gentle on her today, Judy. Too much of that enthusiasm might make her stay home an extra four months," Daniel said jokingly.

"Don't you worry! Got this!" Judy said with confidence.

Daniel hugged Anna and said, "Don't worry about things. You got this, and you'll meet new people with Judy."

"Starting to sound like Mum," Anna said, exasperated.

"Hey. I'm your brother, and I love you. You need me at any time today, you have my class schedule, just come find me. Got it?" Daniel assured her.

"Got it. Thanks," Anna replied with a smile.

"OK, Judy, she's all yours," Daniel said.

"Awesome!" Judy exclaimed happily.

"OK, Anna. Did you want me to walk you to your classes today? So that you can refamiliarize with the school again?" Judy asked.

"That sounds silly, but it would be helpful," Anna said with embarrassment.

"My pleasure. Not silly at all. Plus, I'll introduce you to my friend, Latrice. She's super smart and nice. I think you will like her," Judy said.

"You think everyone is nice, Judy." Anna laughed.

"OK, true, but I think you will still like her," Judy responded joyfully.

"You're so goofy. Thanks for helping me out today. I really do appreciate it," Anna said politely.

"Thanks. I think. And you are very welcome. Come on. Let's get you to class," Judy said.

As the day went on, Anna became placid compared to her nervousness the previous evening. Anna was surprised by the way teachers and classmates welcomed her back. Many wondered what it was like to be home-schooled. Had she made anything else with her gems?

And how were she and William doing? It was like she had never left.

She watched the clock intently. Just five more minutes before the bell rang. She knew that Judy was probably waiting, standing right outside the door. The seconds ticked closer to the twelve, so Anna just picked up her books and started heading toward the door. The bell rang as she passed the teacher's desk, and before anyone could say anything, Anna was in the hallway. Like she suspected, Judy was right there waiting.

"Was it bad?" Judy asked.

"No, it was boring, so I just took off," Anna said plainly.

"Oh, good. I'm glad it's lunch hour. I'm starving!" Judy exclaimed.

"Right?! Me too!" Anna said, agreeing with Judy.

They both grabbed their lunches from their lockers and headed to the lunchroom. Judy saw Latrice straightaway and smiled. After they had bought some milk and juice, they sat at one of the long tables. It wasn't too crowded just yet, so there was enough room for her brother and mates to sit with them. Brandon arrived, sitting next to Judy and Latrice.

"So, how's it going so far?" Daniel asked Anna.

"Good. Boring, but good," Anna replied.

"Well, Brandon, Latrice. This is Anna." Judy was so excited to introduce everyone. She was going to burst if she had to wait any longer. Everyone exchanged their hellos.

"I think my partner, Laurie, has algebra with you," Daniel said to Latrice.

"I'm not sure, maybe. I'm still trying to learn people's names," Latrice replied. She said it politely, but if honesty were in play here, she would only talk to people who struck an interest. Latrice was the type to get bored easily with people.

"Are you the same Latrice that joined my mother's grove?" Anna inquired.

"That would be me," Latrice responded.

"Yeah, um, we're not going to talk about that," Judy said. She gave the silence gesture by putting her finger over her lips.

"Was my mum mean to you?" Anna asked. She would hate to think that her mum was the enemy of her new friend.

"As I said, let us not talk about it. Especially here. Let's just say Latrice is in the grove but under a watchful eye," Judy said.

"Oh my gosh. Now we must know the story," Daniel said. He was fixated on Latrice and wanted to get the scoop. There were times Daniel liked to get a rise out of his mother.

"I'll just say that your mother doesn't like suggestions," Latrice said. There was some sarcasm, but she notably did not want to expound further since she was talking to the high priestess's son and daughter.

"Yeah, she's that way sometimes. You all going to the jubilee or the shut-in?" Daniel asked. He was refraining from talking about his mother and didn't want Anna to be too upset on her first day back.

"Oh, we are going to the jubilee," Judy said. She was forthright enough to answer for all sitting there.

"Well, I guess it's settled, then! Anna, you can hang out with us! I'm sure Judy wouldn't have it any other way," Latrice said. She laughed a bit after giving Judy a bit of a jab.

"I think Laurie and I are going, but she wanted to show me something first. Her and her surprises lately," Daniel said. He rolled his eyes, indicating Laurie always had something to show and tell him later.

"Yeah. I think it will be fun. We all need fun," Anna replied.

Chapter 9

THE JUBILEE

Leaning against the pier rails, Latrice, Judy, Brandon, and Anna stood admiring the water lightly crashing against the rocks below. Seagulls with wings spread allowed the breeze to carry them as though they were conducting a dance. The sun would peek through the clouds periodically to provide a tease of warmth, a sight of the hope that illuminates from the sky. They had almost forgotten how beautiful their country was—vast, luscious green trees and tall blades of bright-green grass, with thistles highlighting it in purple sporadically throughout the land.

"When will William arrive?" Judy asked.

"Should be here shortly," Anna replied.

"Lovely! I can't wait to meet him!" Judy said excitedly.

All of them looked down the pier. People were laughing, walking, or standing along the pier, admiring the oceanview. The carnival was busy by 10:30 that morning.

You could hear people screaming from all the fast rides, kids playing games in hopes of winning big prizes, and laughter. Constant laughter.

"You lot must be from Beith," a lady said.

"What makes you say that?" Latrice asked inquisitively.

"All of you are here enjoying the scenery, admiring the carnival. Many take it for granted," the lady said.

They returned a smile and nodded their heads in agreement.

"We are just always grateful for the town of Goodwin accommodating us every year," Brandon said politely.

"Any chance of finding that altar yet?" the lady asked.

"I wish we could give you a positive answer on the matter, but as of now, Beith is still cursed," Latrice said. She wasn't going to provide the information to a total stranger. Plus, there was still more to investigate, and at that moment, they didn't need outsiders interfering.

"That's too bad. We have our own theories here, but maybe you have already thought of them." The lady pressed on. "Like the Druids there. You have a history of magical Druids that would do ceremonies at some old church there."

"We are aware, but that has already been addressed. We haven't found anything indicating Druids and the shadows," Latrice said. Judy stood with her eyes wide open because the lady seemed to suggest she knew more than what she was saying.

"Too bad. I hope whoever is hiding the altar is soon found," the lady replied.

"I'm sorry. What did you say?" Anna asked.

"The altar. Surely it's hidden. It seems odd that the other altars were found, but yours has not been. Don't you agree?" the lady asked.

Each of them responded, "Yep!" then grinned, wanting to say, *Please, lady, just go away.*

"Well, good luck to all of you. Stay safe. And please, enjoy the festivities. We are all glad you are here," the lady said. Latrice, Anna, Judy, and Brandon all responded with "thank you." Then the lady smiled as she walked away.

"Do you think she knows something we don't?" Judy asked with panic.

"I don't think so. I'm sure it's a common question for everyone. It makes sense that people would be concerned after all this time but probably also fed up with catering to us during these events," Latrice said.

"Everyone seems nice," Brandon said as he shrugged his shoulders.

"Well, let's not think about what-ifs today. There is fun to be had, ladies and gents!" Judy said enthusiastically.

Just then, as people started dissipating from the pier, a tall, handsome man stood gazing upon Anna, holding a single rose. Anna saw him through the people dispersing, and her eyes lit up with excitement and smiled a smile that warmed William's heart. They walked toward each other and embraced with a long kiss.

"Sappy, that one," Brandon said.

Latrice smacked him and rolled her eyes.

"Well, I think it's lovely," Judy said, smiling.

"Of course you would," Brandon replied. Judy gave Brandon a snide grin.

"William, meet my new friends: Latrice, Judy, and Brandon," Anna said.

"Hey. How's it going, mate?" Brandon said as he shook William's hand.

"Great to meet you!" Judy said.

"Hey! Nice to meet you," Latrice said.

"Well, I appreciate you all being kind to Anna," William said as he looked at Anna. He continued. "She's definitely had a rough go at things since her father…well, you know."

"Don't be silly. Of course," Latrice said. Judy and Latrice shared a quick look.

"Well, we didn't come here to stand on the pier all day. Let's go have fun!" Anna joyfully said as she grabbed William's hand.

They all walked toward the carnival and weren't sure what to do first.

"Oh hey. Isn't that Mrs. Swain?" Latrice asked.

"Sure is. Mrs. Swain and some other teachers are here, while the rest are hanging out at the school for the shut-in prom," Judy replied.

"I bet that would have been fun to do as well," Latrice stated.

"If we get back before dark, I'm sure they'll let us in. The principal and the senior class went all out for this one. They set up a movie theater with surround sound speakers in the theater hall. In the hallways, there are carnival games to play. Everyone is going to sleep in the gym. They cleared the shop classes so food vendors could be there since they obviously can't be outside," Judy explained.

"That does sound fun, but I'm glad I'm here instead," William said as he sneaked a kiss with Anna.

"Judy, what would you like to do?" Brandon asked.

"Wannae try the roller coaster?" Judy replied.

"Sure!" Brandon said. Brandon didn't particularly like rides, but if it was a chance to be closer to Judy, he would risk anything.

"Let's meet back here for lunch. Let's say at half twelve?" Anna suggested. Latrice felt like a third wheel.

"Latrice. You comin'?" Brandon asked. Latrice smiled and walked with Judy and Brandon.

Anna and William started walking toward all the games.

"Is this OK, or do you want to do something different?" Anna asked William. She liked the games more than the rides.

"My love, we will do whatever you want. I just want to make sure you are happy and safe," William replied, kissing Anna on her forehead.

"Well, you're important too. You deserve to have fun just as much as I do," Anna said.

"To be honest, I really want to go on that Ferris wheel. I've never seen one that big before and looks fun but scary at the same time," William said.

"Can we go after we meet up for lunch?" Anna asked.

"Sure. There's a huge line there right now anyway. Let me whip ye arse on some of these games, lassie," William said in fun.

"Oh, some competition. OK. You got it!" Anna said.

Everyone was having fun, yet Latrice still felt like a third wheel. She appreciated Brandon and Judy making

161

her feel like she was a part of the "three amigos," but Latrice could tell they wanted some alone time. Brandon made that clear when he gently reached for Judy's hand, and she graciously accepted the gesture. Both Judy and Brandon blushed as they looked at each other. From that moment forward, they were inseparable.

"Hey. I'm going to find Anna and William," Latrice said.

"Oh, they should be by the games. You OK?" Judy asked with concern.

"Yeah, I'm good. You two lovebirds have fun. I have an altar to find," Latrice said, giving a slight grin.

"Just hang out with us. You know, have fun. Give it a rest for one day!" Judy made a desperate attempt to get her to stay. Judy wanted one day when she didn't have to worry about anyone.

"The altar isn't going to find itself. Plus, I feel uneasy. I can't pinpoint it, but something isn't right," Latrice said, alarmed.

"What do you mean?" Brandon asked as he pulled Judy closer to him.

"I'm just saying, I feel something isn't right. Daniel wanted me to meet his girlfriend to discuss the altar and collaborate on ideas," Latrice said. She was feeling a bit annoyed but didn't want to show it. Latrice just wanted to go and see about this potential altar lead.

"Oh, you mean Laurie. Gosh, I haven't seen her at the grove in forever!" Judy exclaimed.

"Maybe that's why she hasn't been there. She has her own theories on where the altar is," Latrice said.

"Well, let's just stay together as much as possible. We'll go with you to find Anna," Judy said firmly.

"OK," Latrice said. All three started heading toward the games area. Then Latrice spotted them throwing darts at the balloons. They briskly walked toward Anna and sneaked up behind her.

"Hey!" Latrice shouted in Anna's ear. Anna jumped and punched Latrice in the arm.

"Ugh! Brat! What's going on with you guys?" Anna's bright smile quickly turned concerned. "What now?" she asked as her shoulders slumped.

"I need to find your brother. He wanted me to meet Laurie about the altar," Latrice said anxiously.

"Let me call him." Anna put her phone on speaker.

William walked up all proud. "Look, love, I got you the bear!"

Everyone but Anna looked at him and gave a slight nod as if to say, "Not now." William looked at Anna, but she didn't notice. Daniel finally answered.

"Anna, you hear me? Reception is shite," Daniel yelled. Anna rolled up her sleeves as the sun's rays encased its warmth upon the city. Latrice's eyes widened, and she gently smacked Judy's arm. Judy looked at Latrice and saw her pointing at Anna's arm. Judy's eyes also widened.

"Where are you? Latrice is looking for you," Anna exclaimed.

"We are by the cave next to the grove," Daniel said. Anna looked at Latrice. Latrice gave a nod indicating she knew where they were.

"OK, she's on her way. Should be there in twenty to thirty minutes."

"Awesome, because I think we found something!" Daniel said enthusiastically.

"OK. Stay safe," Anna said.

"I will," Daniel said before the phone went silent.

"I'll make sure we get home tomorrow and take you guys wherever you need to go," William assured everyone.

"Thank you so much," Anna said humbly. She then noticed the bear. "Aww, thank you for the bear. I love it!"

William kissed Anna. "You are welcome," he said.

"I don't want a kiss, but thank you for driving us about," Brandon said teasingly. Everyone chuckled.

"Are you sure you don't want a kiss, Brandon?" William laughed hysterically.

Latrice had as much fun as she could handle.

"Look familiar, Judy?" Latrice said directly.

"That's the same rune we saw when we looked up runes on your computer," Judy recalled.

"You know something about this? If so, tell me now!" Anna demanded.

"Goodness, Latrice! You're scaring her!" William exclaimed angrily at Latrice as he held Anna.

"I'm sorry, but that's no ordinary rune. That's the all-seeing eye rune, meaning the shapes are directional and the arrows point to the direction of either peace or trouble. You are being used, Anna, and the spirits needed to show you," Latrice explained.

"You mean this was branded on me by the spirits? But I'm not a Druid." Anna tried to wipe her tears away without ruining her makeup. William tried to calm her by rubbing her shoulders.

"No, you are not, but someone close to you is," Latrice stated brusquely.

"What are you suggesting?" Anna glared.

"I'm not suggesting anything. I'm telling you the spirits are trying to protect you and show you at the same time that deception is near you," Latrice said sharply.

"Well, to be fair, that makes sense to me. It turns red when the shadow is in my dreams, but I haven't noticed that any other time," Anna replied. She was soft in her tone but was relieved to get more answers about the rune.

"Let me get out of here to see what Daniel and Laurie are up to. I'll call if we find something," Latrice said. Everyone exchanged hugs and waved goodbye.

"I hope they find something," Brandon said.

"Gotta hand it to her. She is quite ardent in finding the altar. I kinda feel guilty now not going with her," Judy said sadly. Brandon turned Judy to face him gently.

"Well, don't be. Today, we are here to have fun!" Brandon said as he gave her a huge smile.

Judy smiled back and said, "You're right. However, if they find something, and we can get the others from the grove to agree on it, we will call upon the spirits! Sorry, Anna, but the lives of many outweigh those of the few. I refuse to wait on your mother! Speaking of which, there she is." Judy was not backing down on this. She was normally the grove's cheerleader but not today.

"Goodness, love! I love it when you're feisty, but it's scary at the same time. I'm conflicted in my feelings right now," Brandon said hesitantly.

"My mother has protected the grove. If it's true what Latrice said, then the rune would have shown me who that threat was. And it sure as hell didn't show me my mother!" Anna exclaimed.

"Anna, I'm not mad at you, and I'm sorry for sounding like that, but we all have suffered enough. If there is a chance to find this altar finally, then we must act. No one else deserves to die," Judy stated firmly but peacefully.

"No, I totally get it. But if I hear another person try and blame my mum, I will lose my shit!" Anna said.

"Not blaming her for hiding the altar, but maybe a slight blame in keeping us from calling on the spirits," Judy explained.

"Maybe we should stay together just in case," William said. He remembered his promise to Anna, and each time something presented itself about the shadow, he knew he needed to be near Anna as much as possible.

"Good idea, mate," Brandon said plainly.

Agnes and Nancy walked up. Judy looked a little anxious, hoping no one would talk about the rune or anything else.

"Hello, lovelies. Is everyone having fun?" Agnes greeted everyone with a smile and a long sigh as though she were relaxing on a beach somewhere in the States.

"I thought you and Ms. Nancy would be at the school shut-in?" Anna asked.

"Oh no! Too many teens to try and control. I'm too old for that! Plus, I don't need people talking about me and blaming me for something to do with that shadow mess. Isn't that right, Judy?" Agnes said with a sheepish smile.

"Oh, I doubt anyone is really doing that. I think we are all fed up with the curse," Judy said as she looked at Brandon.

"Judy is one of my most grand supporters," Agnes said gleefully, facing Nancy.

"That's kind of you, High Priestess," Judy said quietly.

"Not today. You can call me Mrs. Aird. We are here to relax and have fun!" Agnes declared.

"Absolutely! I think we all needed a break!" Nancy agreed.

"Have you seen Daniel?" Agnes asked.

"I talked to him about fifteen minutes ago. He, Laurie, and soon Latrice are near the grove back in Beith. Why?" Anna asked.

When Agnes listened, she became frozen as though she was in a trance. Judy looked at Brandon.

Anna looked at William.

Everyone instantly became concerned.

"Mum! Are you all right?" Anna asked while shaking Agnes's arm.

"Agnes, Anna asked you a question," Nancy said, touching Agnes's shoulder.

"Yes, yes, sorry. I became overwhelmed with fear. We need to call Daniel and tell him to get home and be safe," Agnes stuttered.

"Jesus! When was the last time she ate?" Anna asked, concerned.

"Early this morning," Nancy said. Anna looked at Nancy as if implying her answer didn't really answer the question.

"There's a seafood restaurant across the way. Let's go there so Ms. Agnes can rest," Brandon stated as he started holding her arm to keep her steady.

"Excellent idea," William agreed as he held the other arm.

Latrice pulled up to the grove and noticed that the thick dark clouds continued to loom. She sat for a few moments, watching the clouds and seeing them shift north very slowly but still moving. That was not common, considering winds move in a southwest position. This heightened Latrice's uneasiness from earlier. She got out of her car, locked the doors, and made her way to the grove. The loch was very calm—no ripples, even with the slight breeze. Daniel and Laurie saw Latrice and yelled for her. Latrice smiled and showed a small sigh of relief.

"Nice to meet you finally. I think you're in one of my classes, right?" Laurie asked while shaking Latrice's hand.

"Yeah, algebra. Nice to meet you as well," Latrice said plainly.

"How's Anna?" Daniel asked.

"Oh, I think she's pretty livid at me after I told her about the rune on her arm," Latrice said.

"Oh shit! What did you say?" Daniel asked while doing a facepalm.

"I told her basically it's a protection rune for the spirits, that the arrows point toward peace or trouble, and that someone close to her may be deceptive. She didn't like that part too well," Latrice said plainly. Latrice wasn't about feelings but about finding this altar, and it was clear that Anna had something to do with it. She wasn't going to stop until she found out what exactly it was.

"What are you saying?" Daniel demanded. Laurie took Daniel's hand and tried to soothe him.

"Daniel, she's here to help."

"I'm saying someone Anna knows, who is likely a Druid, is deceptive," Latrice explained. Daniel hated the notion that it could very well be his mother. Yet he knew Laurie could transform into another person and deceived others, just like he did his sister. He looked at Laurie sternly.

"It could be you. You did deceive Anna in thinking you was some crazy old hag," Daniel said belligerently.

Laurie looked at Daniel with tears flowing steadily down her cheeks.

"I can't believe you said that," Laurie said while greetin' and shaking.

"Look! Both of you—stop! This isn't helping! I'm here because you wanted to show me something and meet Laurie. Let's focus on that for now," Latrice boldly stated. Both Daniel and Laurie agreed. Daniel started to walk toward the cave while Laurie just stood there, taking a moment to herself. Latrice put her arm around her and gave Laurie a slight hug, then whispered, "It will be OK."

They all got to the front of the cave, and there was a symbol on the north side, mirroring the one on Anna's arm, and a single eye.

"Interesting." Latrice stood astute, tilting her head to the side.

"What is it?" Laurie asked excitedly.

"It's two all-seeing eyes that were recently etched here. One is the symbol a Druid would know, and the other a witch would know," Latrice explained.

"How do you know that?" Laurie asked.

With a proud smile, Latrice replied, "Because I am both witch and Druid."

Both Daniel and Laurie looked at each other simultaneously in amazement.

"You're the one I've been waiting to meet! With you here, we can definitely solve this!" Laurie said.

"We found the eyeball on the inside on a dirt wall," Daniel said.

"Show me!" Latrice demanded.

They walked into the cave about twenty-five meters, and on the wall was the witching eye. Latrice touched the eye and quickly saw a vision of the shadow.

"We need to go. Now!" Latrice exclaimed.

As they ran out of the cave, Nixia and the shadow stood behind the wall. But they weren't looking at a solid wall, they were looking through glass.

"Looks like someone is helping them. Is this woman really worth this much hassle?" Nixia asked with disdain.

"She gets what she wants, and I bring souls to your father. She made a blood pact many years ago, and whether or not she wants to believe it's void is on her," the shadow stated plainly. He didn't care as long as he was kept out of the devil's purview.

"Then you need more souls to satisfy my father. He is outraged by your lack of numbers. You are losing ground here and won't get a third chance!" said Nixia intensely.

"Very well, mistress," the shadow said as he bowed to her, and she disappeared from her conjured mist. The shadow realized he had to strike and couldn't wait until darkness. He couldn't bear to lose again and be sent to the Isle of Fire, better known as the Isle of Exile, where useless demons go to burn forever. It infuriated him to think about what could happen if he failed again.

He went into his ghostly form and flew out of the cave like a star shooting across the sky. As he exited the cave, he stared at them. He wanted to take all their lives right then. Instead, he chose Laurie as his victim. Daniel, Laurie, and Latrice looked at the shadow with consternation, as though they were frozen in time. Yet the only one that became frozen was Laurie.

"For your part in the pact you made. You did not choose sides wisely. One can only be true to one but not both," the shadow said. The shadow shot off quicker than a cannon, heading north.

Laurie's horrified silhouette, with her arms stretched out and elbows slightly bent, her face toward where the shadow once was, and her mouth wide open, started to disappear slowly. Pieces of her broke off, starting from the top of her head, and flitted into the air like butterflies delicately flying to a branch. Daniel and Latrice backed away and watched as Laurie passed on. Daniel dropped to his knees, clenched his fists, and screamed as loud as he could. It echoed through Beith like thunder, and the pain he felt was like daggers piercing his chest. Latrice had never seen anything nor heard of anything like that happening before. The loss of her new friend hurt her, but at the same time, she had to think sensibly.

"Daniel, we have to contact Anna and ensure they are OK," Latrice stated.

Daniel acknowledged her and called Anna. No answer. Latrice called Judy. No answer.

"This is not good. We must head back to the jubilee and make sure they are safe," Latrice said.

"Shouldn't we check the cave first? That's where he flew out from!" Daniel said.

"That will have to wait. Our friends need us," Latrice stated.

"You're right!" Daniel said.

Both ran to Latrice's car, and she drove as fast as possible to Goodwin.

"Did you notice that the shadow had a face?" Daniel asked.

"I know you just lost Laurie, but are you daft? No, the shadow didn't have a face!" Latrice exclaimed. Latrice looked at Daniel, puzzled, thinking he was now hallucinating.

"Just think about it for a minute. I swear I'm not daft," Daniel said. He hoped that Latrice would have seen what he saw. The face quickly turned into the shadow's form.

Latrice kept driving.

"No, I'm not seeing it," Latrice said. "Let's just get to Goodwin."

〰〰〰

"Is your phone dead?" Anna asked William.

"Mine is dead too," Judy stated.

"Well, let's head back to the jubilee. Since it looked like a storm or something is coming, maybe they will do the fireworks early!" Judy said. She always had a positive outlook on things. If something went wrong one way, Judy would find a way to lighten any situation.

"Mummy, are you feeling better?" Anna asked.

"Much, thank you. I'm not sure what came over me," Agnes replied.

"Well, thank goodness. You had us worried," Nancy said.

Brandon got up and asked people if their phones were getting reception. All replied no. He rejoined the group to update them.

"Well, it's not just us. Others are having the same issue," Brandon said.

"I'm sure Daniel, Laurie, and Latrice made it home safe. I'll send a text, and it will instantly show on the monitor when the reception comes back," Anna said.

The waiter came to the table and had a disappointed look.

173

"I'm sorry for the interruption, but we can only take cash because the internet is down. I'm sorry for the inconvenience this has caused. Pay at the front if you can or wait until it comes back to pay," the waiter said.

"I got this. Oh, and I don't want any argument about it either," William said. Everyone, including Agnes, didn't say a word, but everyone did render proper gratitude.

"You know my mother will pay you back when we get home, right?" Anna stated. William just giggled and kissed Anna on the forehead.

They got outside, and the jubilee goers seemed more inactive than usual. They looked up at the sky and noticed the clouds were moving north. Toward the front gate to the park, they heard screaming.

"It's the shadow from Beith! Run!" one shouted in horror.

"Everyone, run! Get to safety now!" another yelled.

Just then, the shadow saw Mrs. Swain near a food stand. As Anna and the rest ran up, the shadow swooped down and grabbed Mrs. Swain just like it had done to Anna's father. It covered her eyes and dove straight into the ground.

"We must get back to Beith now so it doesn't take over this town," Brandon said.

"You're right! Let's go!" Anna exclaimed.

As they were running back to their cars, the shadow rose in front of Anna.

"You didn't think you were going to escape, did you? You can thank your mother later. For now, you are mine," the shadow said. The shadow picked up Anna. "Say goodbye, Anna," the shadow said.

"Mum!" Anna screamed.

And in a moment, Anna was gone into the ground. Agnes just stood there. She hadn't reacted when Mrs. Swain or her beloved Anna were taken.

"Agnes! What did you do?" Nancy yelled.

Judy, Brandon, and William were crying, holding each other as they witnessed the death of two important people.

The sun started to appear again in Goodwin. Some continued with the jubilee, and many others went home. Nancy had a firm grip on Agnes's arm while they headed to their cars. Daniel and Latrice saw them and quickly stopped the car and ran up to them.

"What happened?" Latrice asked.

"It's best that we tell you when we're back in Beith. I don't think we are welcome back here anymore," Judy explained.

"Where's Anna?" Daniel asked. Everyone just stood silent. He asked repeatedly and didn't get a response, but they all turned their heads toward Agnes.

"Mum. Where's Anna?" Daniel demanded. He looked at this mother in disgust.

"I didn't want to believe anyone. But my own mother?! I just lost Laurie as well. Why? Why?" Daniel cried.

They headed back to Beith. Not one word was said in each car, but all would be revealed soon enough.

Chapter 10

THE REVEAL

Tuesday after the jubilee, the shock of the shadow killing during the day still imposed despondency throughout the school. Although bright fluorescent lights illuminated the crowded hallways, they felt empty as people walked through them. Jeremy and Christian greeted Daniel when he arrived. Daniel looked at the school and just expressed enormous amounts of dread. Jeremy looked at Christian for support, yet neither of them knew how to comfort Daniel. He had just lost his girlfriend and sister, and there wasn't enough support to cheer him up. Right then, all he wanted to see were Laurie and Anna.

"How are ye holdin' up, mate?" Jeremy asked as he put his arm around Daniel's shoulders.

Daniel had to wait to reply because part of him wanted to say, *How do you think I'm holding up?* but he knew Jeremy was trying to help in his own way. Daniel, with his head facing downward, replied, "I'm OK. I still haven't seen my mum since Saturday. I'm sure she's over at Ms. Nancy's, grieving over Anna. I'll call her when I get home today." His voice was monotone. He felt shattered from all this loss; if he lost one more person, it would end him completely.

"Does Sabrina know?" Christian asked.

"I called my auntie on Sunday, and they both were on the screen. Sabrina screamed. She wouldn't stop screaming. Anna was everything to her. She looked up to Anna, and Sabrina felt profound guilt leaving Beith to be with Auntie after our father died. I told her no one blamed her for leaving. I told her it was the best decision. She wasn't havin' any of that," Daniel explained.

"Oh, I bet," Christian said.

"What happens now with ye?" Jeremy asked.

"Well, I'm going to see Mrs. Turner, Laurie's mum, after school. She didn't believe me when I told her what happened, like how she died, so I'm going to check up on her after school."

"That's cool. Well, if you need anything, just let us know," Jeremy said. Christian nodded in agreement.

They entered the classroom where Mrs. Swain had once taught. Everyone was slumped at their desks, quiet. Too quiet. Mrs. Swain had a rule to have all mobiles in the colored bins before the bell rang. They noticed everyone's phone had been placed in the bins, per instruction. It was out of respect for her. She had taught students to think and not believe everything they hear. Mrs. Swain had believed in her students and cared for all of them. She had been admired by so many; flowers and *I miss you* cards adorned her desk.

The bell was about to ring, yet Mr. Aberdeen, the vice principal, wasn't in the room. Principal Byington appeared on the monitor to give his morning announcement.

"Morning, students. These last few days have been extremely difficult for everyone. We have some counselors volunteering for anyone who may need to talk. Just let your teacher know. If you have something you would like to give in memory of Mrs. Swain, you can bring them to the office or place them around her desk. They will be picked up by the end of the day. On a lighter note, the prom shut-in was a huge success, and I want to thank everyone who participated in setting that up. You know, like me, who had to approve stuff," he said. Some people smirked, some just rolled their eyes, and some students didn't have expressions at all. He continued. "Be flexible, please, as more safety precautions will be coming. Everyone try to have a good day." The screen went black.

"More safety precautions? Wonder how he's going to do that since the shadow can apparently take people during the day," Joseph spouted from the back of the room. "Sorry, Daniel."

"Don't worry about it. I understand and agree with you completely," Daniel replied.

"Good God! Did the shadow take Mr. Aberdeen too?" Don asked with frustration.

Just then, the door swung open. Mr. Aberdeen came in with a new teacher.

"Class, I would like to introduce your new history teacher, Mr. Damien Dougal. He comes to us from Glasgow," Mr. Aberdeen said with a bit of enthusiasm.

"Hello, everyone!" Mr. Dougal said, giving a slight wave and a bright smile.

The young ladies started to sit up straighter in their chairs. Mr. Dougal was slender and built, with short sandy-brown hair that was feathered in the back, deep-blue eyes, the whitest of teeth, and a gorgeous smile. He wore a nice formfitting blue suit with a white shirt, unbuttoned at the top, and black boots that fit under his trousers. You could hear the ladies whisper to each other.

"Oh, I'm goin' to love learning history now," Jacquelyn said as she smirked at the other students.

"OK, calm down, class," Mr. Aberdeen said while rolling his eyes. He whispered to Mr. Dougal, "You have your work cut out for you."

Mr. Dougal smiled. "So I see," Mr. Dougal replied.

"I will leave you to it, then," Mr. Aberdeen said quietly to Mr. Dougal, who smiled and nodded. Mr. Aberdeen left.

Mr. Dougal wrote his name on the whiteboard, *Mr. Dōūgal*, indicating a long vowel sound in his name. He looked at the desk and was annoyed that he couldn't put anything in or on the desk. He had to turn back quickly because his black veins protruded on his neck and face. After a few moments, he turned back around when he felt his face clear. The students looked at each other in bewilderment.

"You OK, Mr. Dougal?" Clarissa asked.

"Yes, thank you for your concern. I have had some health issues lately that I'm trying to get over. Nothing to worry about," Mr. Dougal reassured the class. The class just thought it was first-day jitters.

Mr. Dougal grabbed his large satchel and pulled out blocks of colorful sticky notes. He wrote on the board, *What kind of teacher do you need this year?*

"Class, here is your assignment for the day. Answer the question on the board by writing your answer on a sticky note. Then place the sticky note on the board," Mr. Dougal instructed. "Oh, and please don't write, *Make the assignments easy*," he added.

Some of the students jokingly said, "Ah, that sucks!" One by one, students rose from their desks and walked to the front to retrieve their Post-it Notes. Pink, orange, blue, and green started filling the left side of the board. Mr. Dougal looked at Daniel and asked, "Excuse me, what is your name?"

"Daniel, sir."

"Is there a reason why you don't want to participate?" Mr. Dougal inquired.

"I'm not in a participating mood today," Daniel replied. He was respectful, and when he looked up at Mr. Dougal, Daniel was shocked. He was not expecting the teacher to look like the shadow.

"Is everything all right?" Mr. Dougal asked.

"Um, I need to go see a counselor now," Daniel stated as he grabbed his books and darted out of the room. Christian and Jeremy looked at each other and then ran after Daniel.

"Mr. Dougal, sir. Don't bother trying to get them back. Daniel lost his girlfriend and sister to the shadow this weekend," Jacquelyn said.

"Yeah, and deceptively, his mother was involved as well," Clarissa said. "But it's not for me to tell the story. Daniel would have to tell you," Clarissa concluded.

"Interesting indeed. The mother must be a Druid, I take it?" Mr. Dougal asked, even though he knew the answer to the question.

"Yep. High priestess," Clarissa said while popping her gum.

"Yeah, I'm sure not for long, though," Jacquelyn said.

❧

"Daniel! Where are you goin'?" Jeremy yelled.

"I have to get out of here. You wouldn't understand," Daniel stated. Daniel was looking paranoid, constantly looking around, confirming the shadow wasn't following him.

"Help us understand, mate!" Christian said.

"Mr. Dougal, the new history teacher—I swear on my life that he has the shadow's face!" Daniel exclaimed.

Christian and Jeremy looked at each other and then back at Daniel. They could tell Daniel was serious.

"OK, we want to believe you, but what makes you think that? Sayin' that a teacher looks like or sayin' he's the shadow can get you expelled, mate. You sure?" Jeremy asked.

"I know, but when Laurie, Latrice, and I exited the cave, the shadow flew out from behind us and stared back at us. Trust me, I had time to look at him. I swear, it was like he was in human form that didn't fully transform into the shadow," Daniel explained.

"You sure, mate? I mean, one hundred percent sure?" Jeremy asked. Jeremy looked at Daniel, and the desperation in his eyes confirmed what Jeremy feared.

"What is the bloody thing after, then?" Christian asked.

"Excellent question, and I hope to get answers from Mrs. Turner. That's where I'm going now if you want to come," Daniel stated.

"Oi!" Jeremy let out a sigh. "Let's go, then," Jeremy said.

They headed out to Beith's northwest corner to Blackhorn Drive. Mrs. Turner lived on the end of three semiattached homes.

Daniel rang the doorbell and took a step back. They all could hear some shuffling, then Mrs. Turner greeted them. She had short and wavy sandy-brown hair, light-brown eyes, and freckles on her cheeks and nose.

"Hello, Daniel," she said.

"Hello, Mrs. Turner. These are my mates, Jeremy and Christian. Can we come in?" Daniel asked.

She pushed the lever to open the screen door and allowed them to come in. They took a seat at the dining table.

"Anyone want some tea?" she asked.

"I'll take some, Mrs. Turner," Daniel said.

"Me as well, please, ma'am," Jeremy said.

"Same, ma'am," Christian said.

While they sipped on their fresh black tea, it was awkwardly quiet.

"Daniel, I'm sorry about how I treated you when you told me about Laurie. You were honest with me, and I just didn't want to hear or believe it," Mrs. Turner said. She took a sip of her tea.

"Mrs. Turner, it is OK. We are all trying to understand and heal. We are all hurting in some way, but we still have to find the altar and destroy it. Maybe Laurie left clues. Is it OK if I check her room?" Daniel asked.

"I understand what ye sayin', lad, and I already did. Wait here," she said. She got up, went to the console table, opened the middle drawer, and pulled out two books. One was red and the other white decorated with glitter and the other with doodles. She sat back down and placed them in front of Daniel.

"These are her diaries. She was constantly writing in them," Daniel explained.

"Well, use them and bring them back when you're finished. That's all I ask," Mrs. Turner said with a slight smile.

"Is there anything you can tell us that might help us understand Laurie's connection with the shadow?" Daniel asked.

"I didn't look through her diaries, but I've come to learn that she had special magic. She was sitting where you are now, practicing her transformations. First, it was hair color. Then it was eyes, then the face. That scared me the most. I asked her how she was doing that, and she told me it was given to her as a gift. Druid stuff, she added. Well, it gave me a fright, I tell ye. So I told her not to do that in the house. Had no issue with that nonsense after that," Mrs. Turner stated. She grasped her teacup and tried not to cry, but tears ran down her cheeks silently. Christian, Jeremy, and Daniel all got up and hugged her.

"Thank you so much," she said. She was able to bear a slight smile after the gesture.

"Now, take these and find out what happened to my baby girl."

"One last thing. I know you checked her room, but can we also take a few moments to check? I'm looking for symbols, to be precise," Daniel explained.

"Oh, certainly. Take your time, lads," Mrs. Turner replied.

"Thanks," Daniel said.

They headed upstairs to Laurie's room. The white door with an old brass knob had a wooden plaque marked *Laurie* in the center. The lettering was green, and it had green dragonflies on each side of her name. Daniel opened the door slowly, and a slight creak lingered until he fully opened the door.

"Mrs. Turner was in here for sure," Daniel said.

"Why do you say it like that?" Jeremy asked.

"Because it's clean." Daniel smirked.

There wasn't much to the room: a twin-size bed, a desk with vanity, a dresser, and a few bookshelves. Daniel opened the top drawer of the vanity, only to find makeup stuff. There were three smaller drawers on the left side. One had candlesticks, another some arts and crafts stuff, and the bottom drawer had nothing but a necklace. It had a black cord with an eye charm.

"This is odd," Daniel said.

"It's just a necklace," Christian said.

"Yes, but the charm on it is that of a witch's eye, not a Druid one. Laurie is a Druid. So why would she have this? Plus, this is the same eye that's in the cave," Daniel stated.

"Cave? What are you goin' on about?" Jeremy asked.

"I'll explain everything later, but for now, we need to find Latrice. She's a witch. She would have the answer," Daniel explained.

"That's harsh, dude," Jeremy said.

"No. I mean, she's an actual witch," Daniel said.

They headed downstairs. Daniel was the last out the door and quickly glanced at the room where his love had once slept. He turned and followed his mates.

"Did ye find what you were lookin' for, lad?" Mrs. Turner asked.

"Yes. Thank you again for everything," Daniel said.

He hugged her before leaving. Daniel told Jeremy to head back to school. On the way there, Daniel started reading Laurie's diary.

24 Sept. 2078—Dear Diary. Tonight will be perfect! Full moon! And I will get to meet some new protectors.

25 Sept. 2078—Dear Diary. The blood pact went as expected. Although I was confused about the ceremony. I thought fire from the spirits meant they granted approval, but everything was ice, yet the high priestess said it was OK. It was normal for this type of ceremony, I guess. Catlin was really nice and helpful. Glen from Glasgow wanted to know more on the shadow but agreed to protect people here with his profession. Now we can keep the altar hidden and protect the people.

Daniel began to shake. He couldn't hold the diary, still considering what he just read.

"No way! No fucking way!" Daniel yelled.

"Jesus, mate! What is it?" Jeremy asked.

Christian grabbed the diary from Daniel and read the page.

"Mate. There has got to be an explanation for this. This doesn't make sense!" Christian stated.

"Mind cluin' me in, mate?" Jeremy asked. Jeremy pulled the car over and turned around to face Daniel and Christian. Christian handed Jeremy the diary so he could read for himself. As Jeremy's eyes shifted from line to line, his eyebrows rose in astonishment. When he finished reading, he tossed the book back at Daniel and turned around, facing forward with both hands on the steering wheel. Jeremy punched the steering wheel a couple of times and then exclaimed, "They had us all fooled! I know you didn't know anything about this, Daniel, but damn! Your own mother! I'm sorry," Jeremy yelled. He was filled with so much fury that his eyes were bloodshot, tears filled his eyes, and he covered his face with both hands.

"You and everyone else in Beith have every right to be furious. Nothing to apologize for. Let's get straight first. Then, when you're ready, we need to find Latrice," Daniel said. He could yell or cry. Daniel had become numb at this point and now had to save himself. He knew that he feared he was next to die once he started questioning his mother.

Daniel texted Latrice to see if she could meet them in the car park. The bell rang, and Jeremy saw Latrice running toward them.

"Here she comes now," Jeremy exclaimed.

Latrice sat in the front passenger side. She gave everyone a quick hello and intently looked at Jeremy, then looked at Daniel and Christian.

"OK, you don't look right, and you two look like you're on some old-school Detective Taggart mission. What's going on?" Latrice asked.

"Many things, but first, do you know the meaning of this? I found this in Laurie's room today," Daniel asked.

"It's just a witch's protective eye. It's protecting against evil trying to see you. Why Laurie would have it is anyone's guess," Latrice answered.

"You're goin' to want to read this," Daniel said as he handed the diary to her.

"I knew it! I knew it! I knew it! Since my initiation into the grove, something has been off. I still don't understand why we weren't allowed to call upon the spirits. And this is why!" Latrice exclaimed.

"I haven't read all of it but came across that and thought it was enough to go on. Do you know a Catlin? We are trying to figure out who these other people are," Daniel asked.

"I would really hate to think my auntie had anything to do with this, but I will definitely ask her when I get home," Latrice stated. She paused and sat quietly.

"Oh boy, here comes Judy and Brandon," Daniel said.

Soon, there was a knock on the window on Latrice's side.

"Hey, everyone! What's going on?" Judy asked in her usual cheery voice.

"Oh geez. We need to make our own pact right now. Might as well text William to get him out here as well," Daniel stated while shaking his head.

"What's going on?" Brandon asked.

"Mate, we just need to have those thoroughly involved here before we say anything," Daniel stated.

"I texted William, and he's on his way," Latrice said.

They got out of the car and waited for William. About five minutes later, William arrived.

"Hey, all. What's up?" William asked.

"How are you holdin' up, William?" Judy asked, this time not as cheery but concernedly nonetheless.

"I think we are all trying to cope. I was hoping for some answers on Sunday from Mrs. Aird, but Ms. Nancy said she's not talking due to still being in shock," William said.

"Well, your hope just possibly became a reality. Laurie kept a diary and gave us some clues. Clues we don't particularly like, but clues that involve people we know—starting with my mother," Daniel said. Latrice handed William the diary opened to the entry. William read and started to stumble backward. Brandon got a grip on him to keep him still.

"How far did you read?" William asked.

"Just the first two entries, why? Daniel asked.

"Read this," William stated.

1 Oct. 2078—Dear Diary. As I was praying to the Goddess in the grove, I noticed the high priestess coming out of the cave dressed in all black. Long black dress, a black cloak, and black boots. It looked like she had been there since hours of darkness. After she left, I went to the cave and saw Anna written under the eye on the cave wall.

"Anna's name wasn't there when we were in the cave," Daniel stated.

"Why was Anna taken if the eye was meant to protect her?" Judy asked.

"Seems like someone didn't keep their part of the blood pact, and Anna suffered for it," Latrice proposed.

"Everyone, knowing what we know now, can we all agree to keep this to ourselves until we have all the facts?" Daniel asked.

All agreed.

"Good. Judy, Brandon, it might be best if you accompany Latrice to approach her aunt while me, William, Jeremy, and Christian talk to my mum. Does that sound OK? Then we can meet up at Jeremy's house. It would be mutual ground," Daniel stated.

Again, all agreed. Each had their roles and headed out to their respective places to approach those possibly involved. From each vehicle, only the engine could be heard. No one spoke, and even Judy didn't say anything.

The guys arrived at Ms. Nancy's house first. She saw the car pull up and opened the door as soon as they approached it.

"Is my mum still here?" Daniel asked.

"Yes. Please, come in," Nancy said. Daniel could tell that her politeness was only covering the anger dwelling within her.

"Has she said much?" Daniel asked.

"No, but after the events this weekend, no words need to be spoken," Nancy stated. Nancy folded her arms as she walked toward the family room. Agnes was lying on the couch, propped up with pillows, sipping some tea.

"Oh, Daniel! My sweet Daniel! It's so good to see you. Please forgive me for not being home, but I have barely come to terms with what happened to Anna."

Daniel looked down at the two diaries in his hand and took a deep breath.

"Mum, are you well enough to talk about this weekend? I really need you," Daniel asked. It was more of an act to get his mother's attention and take responsibility for what happened.

"Of course, lad. Anything you need," Agnes replied. She sat up from the pillows, put her tea on its saucer, and had a slight smile on her face. She was not prepared for what was coming.

"Mum, just before Anna was taken, Laurie was killed by the shadow. I went to her house today and talked with Mrs. Turner, and she gave me two of Laurie's diaries," Daniel began. He looked at his mates for encouragement, then looked back at his mum.

"What do you know about the blood pact, Mum?" Daniel asked. His voice was stern, and he wasn't there for guessing games. He wanted the truth. Agnes's folded hands clenched, and her smile turned contrite.

"Oh, a blood pact? Was this part of your 'this and that' you are always telling me about?" Nancy yelled.

"Sweetheart, please, come sit down. It's checkmate. She will have to explain," John stated. He had known this day would come and was pretty calm about it. He had to be for Nancy.

Agnes took a deep breath, and tears filled her eyes.

"I was a little girl. Something happened between my granny and my auntie where their blood pact became void, but not between them and the spirit. When that happened, my aunt wanted to keep Druids in the family, dark druidism that is; so, she told me that if I signed my name in blood, I could be a powerful high priestess. Yet these Druid powers my aunt spoke of I really didn't have. I tried fervently to learn the ways of the Druid but only bestowed certain powers upon me. So, when it was time for the spirits to announce the new high priestess, I was the only one running for the position, so to speak, and got it by default. Not anything the spirits did," Agnes said.

Everyone just sat there. Nancy was in her chair quietly crying, shaking her head in disbelief, while William wanted to tear into Agnes, who would have been his future mother-in-law had she not killed his beloved. Daniel saw William's anger, gently grabbed his wrist, and shook his head no.

"When did you start talking to the shadow?" Daniel asked.

"It wasn't until I got married that the shadow approached me and demanded more sacrifices. The blood pact I made when I was little wasn't void just because of my age. So in secret, I had to go to the altar and worship the dark king to keep you safe during daylight hours. Failure to do so brought out the shadow at his own time," Agnes stated.

"So what was the point between you and these other people? How do you know them?" Daniel demanded.

"Mr. Stone contacted me because I'm the high priestess, and he wanted information on the shadow from a Druid's point of view. Laurie was already in my grove, and I convinced her that a blood pact was necessary to protect the people in Beith. Catlin is a mage, and she wanted to protect her niece. Yet in order to do this, to keep their business and families safe, it meant worshipping the dark king. When no one worshipped the dark king, the shadow had free rein during the day and night," Agnes stated.

"What about these runes?" Daniel asked.

"I wanted to protect Anna, especially since she was in contact with the shadow when it took your father. So, for her protection, I asked the spirits to protect her. The atrocities happening in Beith are my fault but not hers. However, the shadow thought I put a protection rune on her, so in retaliation, it took her," Agnes stated. She placed her hands over her face and cried. There was nothing more she could say that could make this treachery disappear.

"Get her out of my house. I never want to speak to her again!" Nancy stated.

While Agnes was telling her story, John had already gone upstairs to pack Agnes's belongings and brought them downstairs. Daniel took his mother by the hand and grabbed her bags and walked to their house.

"Thank you, Ms. Nancy, for everything. Trust me, no one feels more betrayed than I do," Daniel said.

"I doubt that very much. I think Anna would have a say in that if she were here. Yet I don't envy your situation, Daniel. If you or Sabrina need anything that doesn't have to do with her, then I will be there. Agnes betrayed us all, and I can't be a friend to someone that does that kind of betrayal. God could not give me enough time to forgive her," Nancy stated. She wanted Agnes to see her anger, feel her anger, and know that once that door shut behind them, Agnes was no longer welcome. The damage had been done, and there was no going back.

"Give me a second, guys," Daniel said. Jeremy, William, and Christian were more than happy to oblige. William thought about Anna so much that he retched up everything in the flower bed. Jeremy and William didn't even take the mickey out of him because it was a natural response after what they had heard.

Daniel and Agnes walked into their house, and Daniel quietly placed her bags by the staircase. Daniel stood in disbelief.

"How could you? After Dad died, I was left to fill the father role, but who was around to keep me safe? Clearly not you! You're my mother, but I hate you and love you at the same time! That can't be normal! You lied and manipulated people so that you could keep whatever Druid nature power so you could remain high priestess. You didn't have the courage to sacrifice yourself so others could live.

You will pay for what you have done, and I won't be here to see it," Daniel yelled.

"Daniel, please don't…," Agnes begged.

"No, Mum! You made it very clear who you are for, and you are for yourself. I hope you can live with that," Daniel said.

Agnes tried and plead with Daniel, but he ignored her. He grabbed some of his things and headed out the door. Tomorrow, the day of reckoning would come.

Chapter 11

THE DESTRUCTION

Latrice arrived home with Judy and Brandon by her side.

"I'm sure your auntie has nothing to do with this," Judy assured.

"Let's hope not," Latrice replied.

"Aunt Catlin! Are you home?" Latrice yelled.

Catlin came from her room.

"What is it, dear?" Catlin asked. She could see in Latrice's eyes that there was cause for concern.

"Please tell me that you weren't part of some blood pact with Mrs. Aird. If you were, I need to hear everything now!" Latrice demanded.

"I was afraid this day would come," Catlin said. "Please, let's sit in the family room."

Judy and Brandon sat on the sofa, Latrice in the recliner, and Catlin on the couch.

All eyes were on Catlin.

Judy could see the anger brewing on Latrice's face.

"The main premise that Mrs. Aird described was to form a blood pact to outwit the shadow, or the doctor, as I call him. None of us wanted to worship the dark king, so we tried to devise ways for us specifically not to. Dr. Stone only did so to keep his psychology practice from failing. From what I read in the news, his building burned down with him in it on Friday. Anyway, the pact was formed to keep everyone safe while we do the dirty work. The problem was people didn't keep their promise to the shadow to worship the dark king. The given powers were fading, and well, you know the rest," Catlin said.

"How could you keep this from me? You know I don't need protecting!" Latrice yelled.

"You are a witch and a Druid. All the more reason to do anything to keep you safe," Catlin replied.

"So, you knew about the altar as well?" Latrice asked.

"Yes, I did. Although I only knew of its existence two years ago, it still doesn't excuse me not saying anything about it," Catlin said.

"Auntie, we have had four people die since you knew," Latrice said.

"Six," Judy corrected. "Anna, her father, Anna's uncle, Mrs. Swain, Laurie, and Brandon's sister."

"Mrs. Aird assured us that everyone would be safe as long as we made the blood pact," Catlin said.

"You know we have to go to the councillor tomorrow on this, right?" Latrice exclaimed.

"Yes, I'm willing to take full responsibility for this," Catlin said.

"Why do you call him the doctor?" Latrice asked.

"I've only talked to him on the phone and never seen him in human form, but he has a doctorate in anthropology," Catlin explained.

"Wait. You mean to tell me the shadow is human?" Latrice asked.

"No. Not exactly. He is a demon that can transform into a human if needed," Catlin stated.

"Oh my god. I didn't believe Daniel when he told me the other day that the shadow looked human as it flew out of the cave," Latrice said.

"How did you discover all this?" Catlin asked.

"Laurie kept diaries, and we found some entries dating back to 2078. We will be at Jeremy's tonight as we need a plan for tomorrow. I need to be away from here to process that you, Auntie, was part of this blood-pact thing. Unless it's me, I strongly suggest not answering the phone," Latrice said. For possibly the first time, Latrice was at a loss for words. She started pacing back and forth, controlling her breathing while packing her backpack.

"I love you, Auntie, but I'm hurt, furious, and sad, and I don't want to do something that might hurt you. That's why I have to be somewhere else tonight," Latrice said.

"I understand," Catlin said.

They each exchanged a hug, and the three left for Jeremy's house. Catlin was so angry that she randomly turned things to ice, her one mage ability she used to relieve stress. Catlin went to her monitor and called Agnes, but Agnes didn't answer. Catlin knew she deserved to die. It wouldn't replace the lives lost, but knowing the altar's location and not doing anything about it was something only karma would render her times three. And that was worse than a swift death.

Latrice, Judy, and Brandon made it to Jeremy's house just before the sun went down.

"What did you find out?" Daniel asked.

Before Latrice could answer, Jeremy's mum walked into the room.

"Jeremy, you didn't tell me we were going to have company," Jeremy's mum said.

"I'm sorry, Mum, but this is really important, and all will be revealed tomorrow. We just can't risk information secretly sent out too early," Jeremy stated.

"So you don't trust me? I promise, whatever it is, I won't say a word," Jeremy's mum stated. She put her hand over her heart to visually show her promise.

"Your mum does work at the councillor's office, Jeremy. She could help us," Christian said.

"Good point," Jeremy replied.

"You can't just come to the councillor's office without an appointment. I mean, unless you found the altar, there are other matters the councillor is currently addressing," Jeremy's mum said.

Everyone looked at Jeremy's mum. Each one had an expression of grief and determination.

"Oh my. This is going to be a long night. I will get you in to see the councillor in the morning. I just bought a bunch of frozen pizzas. Is that OK?" Jeremy's mum asked.

"That's perfect, Mum. Thanks," Jeremy replied.

Jeremy's mum wasn't sure how to feel. She walked into the kitchen and turned on the oven. She stood near the corner of the oven, staring at the floor.

"I know what you're thinking, Mum. We know where the altar is, and we need the councillor's permission to destroy it. Plus, Daniel's mum was hiding it all these years. The king gave his authority for proper punishment if that were to occur," Jeremy stated.

Jeremy's mum didn't say a word. She turned around and preheated the oven.

"There are Cokes and Irn-Brus in the cabinet. Take as much as you wish."

"Oh, but wait. There's more. My auntie was in on the blood pact because she was told it would protect the citizens of Beith if they worshipped some dark king. She knew about the altar as well for the past two years," Latrice stated. Her tone was sarcastic and with ire.

"She lied. She lied to all of us!" William exclaimed.

Judy went to comfort William. Then Brandon went over to put his arm around him. At that moment, William just let it flow. Jeremy's mum came over to hold him a bit.

"Come, come, lad. It's OK." She looked at all of them while holding William. "We will make this right tomorrow," Jeremy's mum asserted.

Everyone was waking up, and Jeremy's mum already had a feast like those in a luxurious hotel displayed. Beans, mushrooms, eggs, toast, fruit, black pudding, sausages, and tomatoes filled the countertops.

"Mum. You went all out! Why?" Jeremy asked. Everyone was so grateful for the food and filled their plates one by one.

"That. That right there is why," Jeremy's mum said.

She pointed to all the smiling faces. She continued. "When was the last time all of you had a decent meal?"

Before Brandon mentioned the seafood restaurant in Goodwin, Judy stated, "It has been a while, ma'am. Thank you for this." Judy looked at Brandon, motioning for him not to say anything. The last thing anyone needed was a reminder of the day Anna and Laurie were killed.

"We need all the energy we can get for today," Jeremy's mum stated.

"I say we all go home, freshen up a bit, then head to the councillor's office by, let's say, half nine?" Judy directed.

"Brilliant idea. Give us time to make sure certain individuals are ready and present to the councillor," Jeremy's mum stated.

"Again, no word of this until we talk to the councillor. Nothing is certain until the altar is destroyed!" Daniel said.

Everyone responded with "agreed" and left for their respective homes. Latrice dropped off Brandon and Judy, then went home to face Catlin. As she walked through the front door, the atmosphere was dark. She noticed file folders on the counter, and when she opened each one, she saw the house, car, and bank accounts were all in Latrice's name.

"Auntie! What is all this paperwork for?" Latrice asked as she walked briskly toward Catlin's room. She knocked on the door.

"Auntie!" Latrice yelled. Then she turned the handle and noticed Catlin lying in bed. Latrice became frantic and shook Catlin to wake her, but she didn't move. Latrice called an ambulance, and about ten minutes later, the paramedics arrived and performed CPR. Latrice was standing in the corner of the room, watching intensely, hoping to revive her. After twenty minutes, the medical service personnel removed their equipment and respectfully placed a sheet over Catlin's body.

"I'm sorry, love. We will call the coroner for ye. Is there anyone else we can call for ye?" the medical examiner asked.

"No, no, thank you." Latrice sobbed. She dropped to her knees and cried. Latrice went over to Catlin's body to check for visible wounds. Catlin looked like she had died in peace. Latrice knew by looking at her that Catlin had released her mage powers to avoid the harsh karma she would have received if she had stayed alive. Catlin understood a life for a life and felt the most respectful way to honor those that died because of her involvement was to die herself. Latrice reached for her phone to call Judy.

"Judy, if you are ready early, could you and Brandon come over, or do you need me to pick you up?" Latrice asked.

"Latrice! Is everything OK? Why are you greetin'?" Judy exclaimed.

"Catlin is dead," Latrice stated. She tried to hold back the tears but couldn't stop.

"I'll get Brandon to drive, and we will be right there!" Judy stated.

Latrice just sat next to the dresser with her arms around her bent legs. As each moment passed, she still hoped that her auntie would wake up. Latrice went back to the kitchen to look at all the files. Most of the files' dates were three days after the blood pact. *She knew this would happen.* Latrice found the last will and testament of Catlin Beaumont. Latrice skimmed through it and realized what her auntie wanted.

The coroner arrived and took the body to Stephen's Serenity Funeral Home. Judy and Brandon arrived a few moments after he left. Judy saw the front door wide open and instantly panicked.

"Latrice! Latrice!" Judy yelled as she and Brandon walked through the house. Then Judy saw her on the floor, staring off into another world.

"Latrice. What happened?" Judy asked.

"Not sure. But she was dead when I got here. Emergency medical came and did CPR, and the coroner just left with her body." She looked up at Judy. "She was all I had," Latrice said.

"We must get going to the councillor's office. Why don't you stay and rest," Judy said.

"No, this is too important. I must go," Latrice replied. She quickly washed her face, put on some deodorant, and immediately left. While driving, Latrice received a call from Daniel.

"Hey, we're all here. How far away are you guys?" Daniel asked.

"We are only a few minutes away. I'm not going to explain everything, but my aunt died last night," Latrice said.

"What? She was our only other living witness! I mean, I'm sorry Latrice. I really am," Daniel said. He was incensed to say the least. He needed everyone there.

"No, I understand. I just hope that we can get all of this behind us soon," Latrice said.

"Same here. Again, I'm really sorry. See you when you get here," Daniel said as they simultaneously hung up their mobiles.

"What did he say?" Judy asked.

"They're waiting on us, basically," Latrice said.

"Well, there it is. The North Ayrshire Councillor's Office," Judy said as she pointed to a small brick building.

"Now that everyone's here, let me address the councillor, and I'll come get you when he's ready for an audience," Jeremy's mum said.

They watched as Jeremy's mum walked into the office, and it wasn't two minutes later when the door swung open, and there stood Councillor Mark MacDannels. He was a slender man with snow-white hair cut short and a matching perfectly trimmed beard and mustache. That day he wore a black, with very minuscule yellow pinstripes, blazer and matching trousers.

"Please, please, come in!" Councillor MacDannels said. He waved them into his office. "Please, shut the door. Have a seat, all of you. Am I hearing this correctly that you have found the altar?" he asked.

He couldn't sit down. He had to hear it for himself.

"Yes, sir, and my mother is behind it all," Daniel said.

The councillor stood in amazement, watching a child bring his mother to her indubitable fate. One by one, each stood in front of the councillor and gave their account of what had happened—showing pictures of the cave, the protection runes, footage from Goodwin during the jubilee, the diaries, and Mr. Dougal as possibly the shadow in human form. Luckily for everyone present, the councillor understood that this particular town was dealing with something other than ordinary. Councillor MacDannels went from standing to sitting in this plush leather chair, elbows on his desk and hands folded. As he heard each account, he kept his composure, but his eyes were glassed over with fervency. The final account was Agnes's testimony. Jeremy's mum called the police and the police brought her to the councillor's office.

"Mrs. Aird, I cannae say anything you haven't already heard from these brave children. You have a right to state your testimony, but I am duly inclined to sentence you now," Councillor MacDannels stated.

"Everything the children stated is true. No discrepancies. I am fully aware that I am undoubtably responsible, regardless of those involved in the blood pact. May their names be written as innocent," Agnes stated.

"We cannae speak for Dr. Stone, but my auntie and Laurie—I plead with you, Councillor, that they be held innocent," Latrice begged.

"The citizens of Beith have been waiting for this liberation for decades. Innocent lives lost, from wee ones to your very own loved ones and friends. Are we for certain that once the altar is destroyed, Beith is free from the curse?" he asked.

"Yes, Councillor, as long as the altar is torn down and buried in the deconsecrated ground," Latrice stated.

"Then I leave you in charge of the altar's destruction, Ms. Beaumont. In the meantime, Mrs. Aird, until I talk to the king directly, you have been found guilty of seventy-five counts of second-degree murder and sentenced to house arrest. You may be on your property and are allowed to vacate your residence for emergency purposes only. Do you understand your sentencing as described to you, Mrs. Aird?" Councillor MacDannels asked.

"Yes, Councillor," Agnes replied.

Councillor MacDannels then pushed a button on his phone, and two officers quickly entered.

"Please take Mrs. Aird to her residence as she is on house arrest," Councillor MacDannels stated. He saw the officers about to cuff her, and he interrupted. "No need for that, but thank you, officers," he said.

Daniel watched as they took his mother out of the room. Her arm would be injected with a sensor, which would ping authorities if she moved off her property.

"As far as your aunt, Ms. Catlin Beaumont, and Miss Laurie Turner, they will be written as innocent parties," he said.

"Thank you!" both Latrice and Daniel said. It took enormous restraint not to jump up and down and scream with gladness.

"What I would like to see happen now is the destruction of the altar before making a public announcement. I want to eliminate room for error. What would you need help with to accomplish this, Miss Beaumont?" the councillor asked.

"I would need a few contractors to move the altar pieces to the old church, some pickaxes to tear down the wall, and a demolition crew to destroy the cave," Latrice said.

"Margorie…," Councillor MacDannels started to request, but she interrupted.

"Already on it, sir," she said. She was so proud of her son and his friends that she, too, wanted to leap for joy.

"Very well then. Please give the officers directions to this location, and we will start this now," Councillor MacDannels stated. With a jagged smile, he added, "You don't have to be so proper now."

They got to the foyer, looked at each other briefly, then screamed and jumped for joy. They exchanged hugs and shared tears of joy.

They ran to their vehicles and headed to the cave. The mini convoy of construction vehicles, trucks, and police cars gathered the town's attention. People walked behind the group of vehicles and asked what was happening. No one knew, and those in the convoy didn't respond, per the councillor's orders. This was the proper moment for the weans. They had earned it.

The convoy stopped near the grove. The construction team was on standby to receive Latrice's order. The proud moment came when Daniel, Latrice, Judy, Brandon, William, Christian, and Jeremy each grabbed a pickaxe and headed to the cave. The eye, once centered on the wall, no longer showed.

"Daniel, it would be an honor for you to take the first strike," Latrice said with a smile.

Daniel looked at the wall, took the axe, and slammed it into the wall.

"For Father!" Daniel yelled.

"For Anna!" William yelled.

"For my auntie!" Latrice screamed. When her axe struck the wall, not only did the cave shake, but rubble and glass hit the ground. Each of them quickly backed away and waited a bit for the dust to clear.

Meanwhile, in the netherworld, the shadow and Nixia stood before the dark king.

"Do you hear that? Each strike is another reminder of your failure. You were so worried about those humans keeping their pact with you that you didn't keep your pact with the dark king," Nixia vituperated.

Each time the axe hit a rock or removed pieces of rubble, the dark king's altar area, where he sat, shook.

"Father, send him to exile!" Nixia demanded. "I am thirsty to see him devoured in flames."

The dark king took the shadow and put him in human form. He ensured the shadow was dressed in a tuxedo with twenty-four-karat-gold cuff links, a bow tie, and shiny black Giuseppe Zanotti loafers. The shadow knelt. "Thank you, dark king, for your forgiveness and this gift."

In a growling, deep voice, the dark king responded, "I don't believe in forgiveness, and I don't give things without a purpose. You will be the best dressed in the Isle of Exile. Enjoy your eternal stay."

"Please! Please! I'll do anything!" the shadow shrieked. Nixia licked her lips and gave a sinister smile because she knew what was coming next. Just then, the area where the shadow was standing opened, and he fell to the Isle of Exile. The screams bellowed throughout the netherworld as those sent before the shadow were burned for eternity.

"What shall we do now, Father? Send me! I will gather all their souls for you," Nixia stated.

The dark king sat quietly for a moment and gazed upon her. He stood up from his fiery throne, walked down the ramp toward her, and said, "Not yet, my child. I will allow the curse to be removed for now. However, when a human signs their name in blood, I expect payment." He caressed her cheek and said, "And I will get my payment."

Nixia smiled, anticipating her father's deviant plan.

They could see the altar as they cleared more of the rubble and glass. Latrice called on the contractors to help move the five pieces of sandstone from the ten-by-ten-square-foot opening. There was a square slab for the base, two equal-sized rectangular slabs for the sides, one slab that kept the two rectangular pieces in place, and one long slab with demonic symbols on it. The whole assembly resembled a single prayer kneeling bench.

"I am not even going to try and guess what those mean. Right now, I really don't care," Latrice said.

"I heard that!" Brandon said, agreeing with Latrice.

As they placed the pieces in trucks, more onlookers surrounded the site. One onlooker exclaimed, "Oh my god! I think they found the altar! Look at those slabs!"

Officers instilled order at the site.

Latrice then went up to the road to address the people.

"Citizens of Beith, I am Latrice Beaumont. I am the lead excavator for this site. There will be a public announcement by the councillor here in a few hours with information that has transpired from the last few days. I ask that you allow us time to tend to this area and do what we need to keep everyone safe. Thank you," Latrice stated.

Onlookers did move back from the road. Others went home to wait for the announcement, and a few older gentlemen hypothesized about the slabs and how they had gotten there.

"Miss, the rubble and the slabs have been removed. Some of the forensic officers took before-and-after pictures of the site, and the cave is destroyed so no entry can be permitted," one of the contractors said.

"Thank you so much! We must take the slabs to the old church so they can be buried there," Latrice said.

"I'll ring in the dimensions of the slabs so the team can start working on grave sites now," the contractor stated.

"Perfect! Thank you! Do you know how long that will take?" Latrice asked.

"Shouldn't take but about an hour, miss," he said.

"OK, we will meet you up there," Latrice replied.

The contractor nodded, and the construction workers headed to the old church.

They stood to look at the cave, not saying a word.

"I know this is not where they died, but maybe we can gather some flowers and place them here in memory of them. Turn this place of evil into a place of peace. What do you think?" Judy asked.

"Sounds like a lovely idea," William said.

Each of them went around the loch, picking up wildflowers: pink geraniums, mini violet pansies, knotgrass, and shepherd's purse.

"Sometimes, I would dream about Anna. She is wearing a flowing blue dress, her hair flowing through the breeze, and she's dancing and smiling. I would like to think she is free, happy, and at peace wherever she is," William said. He placed the large bouquet at the old cave's entrance.

"That's beautiful, William," Judy said as she lightly rubbed his back for comfort.

"For my sister, Caroline. The pictures at the house with her smiling and doing some craft thing. She always wanted to paint a picture for me. I miss having her around," Brandon said.

After Brandon placed his bouquet, Judy went to hold Brandon. They exchanged a quick, sweet kiss. Brandon smiled at Judy in appreciation.

"I'm going to wait until my aunt's funeral. Too much has happened today, and we're not in the clear yet," Latrice said.

"I understand completely," Judy said.

"Let's go to the hill," Jeremy said.

When they got to their cars, a few sunrays peeked through the clouds and glistened on the loch. Latrice smiled slightly as though acknowledging something telling her to hang on.

They got to the church and prepared the ground for the stones.

"What do we do? We don't have a priest," Judy asked.

"Well, this is kinda different. This came from something sinister rather than something holy. I will bind the stones to the earth. Trust me, it's not a big ceremony or anything."

The largest of the stone slabs was placed first in the ground.

There was a lantern at the front of the site. If it became lit, it meant the spirits approved and kept that stone from doing harm.

"I bind this stone and any associated entities to the earth. It can no longer cause harm to people or be used again for any purpose. Sacred spirits, I ask your favour in binding this stone," Latrice said.

Her voice was steady. The lantern was lit with fire by the spirits. Latrice did the same spell for each of the stones, and the sky opened completely when she finished the last one. Only a few clouds floated across the sky. There were cheers, but many weren't positive about why the sky had opened up or why a young girl was burying large slabs of stone. All they knew was that it seemed important and something good came from it.

"We have to get to Councillor MacDannels and let him know everything is complete," Latrice said.

When they arrived back at the building, some news crews were present.

"What are they doing here?" Daniel asked.

"Someone must have leaked something because there's Jessica McGowen," Latrice said.

She followed in her mother's footsteps, which Stephanie would be very proud of her if she were alive today. As they got out of the cars and rushed to the building, one of the news reporters ran alongside them, asking, "Is it true that they found the altar?"

Jeremy's mum was waiting for them and hurried them into the councillor's office.

"Sir, I swear, we did not say anything to anyone," Latrice said.

"Oh, I know. Not much action happens here, so when your excavation started, people were already assuming that's what it was. We need to make that announcement now," Councillor MacDannels said. He sat at his desk, and they all stood behind him. With a push of a button, all televised stations were interrupted. Each monitor in every home and office was to witness history.

"Hello. Today, I am happy to tell you that Beith no longer lives under a curse. These weans—or shall I say young men and women—were able to procure the altar's location through their intuition, foresight, and their special abilities. Through careful consideration of the evidence presented to me this morning, Mrs. Agnes Aird was arrested for seventy-five counts of second-degree murder and has been put on house arrest until the king provides further instruction. Beith owes these young people a huge amount of gratitude. They experienced their own loss of friends and family, yet they continued seeking answers to free us all from the malevolent curse. You see them with me: Latrice Beaumont, Daniel Aird, Judy Lochland, Brandon Hensworth, Jeremy Tucker, William Calahagn, and Christian Doyle. This day, the seventh of October, 2080, will forever be marked as the day of Beith's liberation," Councillor MacDannels stated.

"Thank you so much, sir. I think I can speak for all of us in saying that we appreciate you and your help today," Latrice said.

"Absolutely. Now, go home! Celebrate as much as you can. I know today has been a mix of sorrow and joy, but you have all earned your honour today." Councillor MacDannels smiled and walked them out of the building.

"Guys, I have to tell you something," Daniel said. He was hesitant but knew he had to tell them now rather than later.

"What now?" Jeremy asked. He was bracing himself for the next bad news.

"Look. I'm going to celebrate with you, but I already texted my aunt, and I'm moving to Edinburgh to be with Sabrina. You guys have been there for me, and I will miss you, but you can always come to visit. I hope you understand," Daniel said.

"Oh, you are not leaving here until we get wrecked, mate!" Jeremy said. Daniel and Christian laughed yet agreed.

"OK, but at your house. I sure as hell don't want to be on house arrest with my mum," Daniel said.

"Wow!" Latrice said.

"Too soon?" Daniel said.

"She's still your mum," Judy said. She looked at Daniel with a bit of disappointment.

"Sorry, you're right. I'm just all over the place right now, and I'm not going to heal if I'm here with my mum," Daniel said.

"I know," Judy said and hugged Daniel.

Chapter 12

ABOVE THE SHADOWS

For the first time in decades, the sun was much brighter, the rays spread further, and the weight of any darkness lifted. Beith was finally free from the control of the shadow's grip. A town that had been taught to fear the darkness didn't have to fear anymore. Many people didn't know how to react to this newfound freedom and still believed they were not fully in the clear of the shadows. Others couldn't wait to have late-night get-togethers, barbecues, movie nights, and whatever fun they missed out on. It was Beith's time to shine. News traveled fast throughout Scotland about the altar having been found, destroyed, and buried. Even Glasgow's very own Jessica McGowen wanted to cover the story, especially at night.

"Jessica McGowen here, surrounded by many residents of Beith. Just look at their smiling faces, Dave!" she exclaimed.

"When did the residents there realize they were safe?" Dave from the WCTV newsroom asked.

"Early this morning," McGowen said.

"Did they finally know the reason why the altar was there in the first place?" Dave asked.

"Excellent question, Dave. I was told when I first arrived that the high priestess of the Druid grove here—and I'm told her name is Agnes Aird—was keeping the altar hidden because many years ago she made a deal with devil. In order to keep her magic, she had to sacrifice her family and friends to the shadows," she stated.

"Wow! Unbelievable!" Dave said. His shook his head back and forth.

"Dave, I have one of her closest mates here. Let's ask her," she responded. "Nancy, when did you first realize Agnes was hiding a secret?" Jessica McGowen asked.

"Great question. I always thought there was something off about Agnes but always attributed it to her being a high priestess, and things always seemed so secretive. I guess it was during the jubilee when Mrs. Swain, the history teacher, was taken by the shadow, and Agnes seemed unfazed. Yet she went into complete shock over her daughter, Anna, being taken by the shadow," Nancy said calmly.

"The big question now is, are you still going to be mates?" Jessica McGowen asked.

Nancy stood there for a moment, and the camera zoomed in on her face. You could see Nancy's eyes start filling up with tears, and then she said harshly, "She used us for a power that many cannot comprehend. She kept this town in fear for selfish reasons. The shadow siphoned its strength from her daughter, Anna, and she went through so much pain, and for the sake of what?" Nancy started to get fervent as her voice got louder and louder.

"I cannot be mates with someone who only cares about themselves," Nancy said. Her husband put his arms around her shoulders and motioned her to get out of the camera's view.

"Dave, I think the town of Beith has had their fair share of mourning, pain, and heartbreak. I want to thank Nancy for sharing her thoughts," Jessica McGowen said.

"Wow. What a powerful message. We are definitely feeling that over here at the news station, Jessica," Dave said with stupefaction on his face.

"I know, Dave. But we have other folks here who are dying to share their thoughts on the freedom of Beith!" Jessica said, smiling. Loud cheers could be heard in the background. Everyone could be seen waving into the camera, laughing, smiling.

"Jessica, can we confirm that the altar is actually destroyed?" Dave asked.

"Yes, Dave. From what I was told earlier, it was in a cave near the grove. They tore down the wall, and there it was. A small altar made of stone. Some of the Druids and their friends used pickaxes and assistance from contractors to knock it down. They then removed each stone, one by one, and buried each one. Remarkable what they did, Dave," McGowen said.

"That is amazing! I'm sure Beith, along with all of Scotland, is celebrating!" Dave stated.

"Absolutely, Dave. We have some of the heroes here! What are your names?" she asked.

"Latrice," Latrice said quickly.

"I'm Judy!" Judy exclaimed.

"I'm Brandon," Brandon said plainly.

"I can just see it on your faces and with this crowd!" McGowen said. The crowd cheered loudly again. Someone in the background popped a champagne bottle and started spraying it all over everyone. Tumultuous cheers sounded and echoed through the streets as the camera continued to scan, showing people grilling in their driveways and playing kickball in the street.

"First of all, thank you all for your bravery! Latrice, I'm going to direct this to you since you headed up the excavation. How does it feel to be part of Beith's history?" McGowen asked.

"I don't think any of us really felt we did this for a page in a history book. We have experienced what most of Scotland has not, and we were determined to rid the evil and just be normal again," Latrice stated.

"I heard humility and selflessness. That was well said," McGowen said. She placed her hand over her heart and felt proud.

"I think many could learn from that. Wonderful state-ment," Dave said.

"Exactly. But, Dave, I think it's time to get back to the festivities here in Beith!" McGowen said. The camera panned to all three again.

"Are you three excited like everyone here?" McGowen asked.

Simultaneously all three said, "YES!"

Brandon had a melancholy look upon his face. He wanted to be excited with everyone else but couldn't. All he could think about was losing his sister to the shadow. McGowen picked up immediately on his emotion and waited a little bit before addressing him.

"What changes do you think will happen in Beith, now that everyone is free?" McGowen asked.

"Well, we do have one exciting news," Judy said, giggling. She wasn't sure if she should say anything quite yet. Judy looked at Latrice to get approval.

"Goodness, mate, tell the world already!" Latrice said.

"Oh good. I was about to burst! The Druids here are going to hold a special ceremony to elect our new high priestess," Judy said with excitement.

"Do you feel that Beith will welcome that, considering it was a high priestess that hid the altar?" McGowen asked.

Latrice stepped in and responded. "There are a few things that are happening here. Clearly, there was a higher power that orchestrated the movements to reveal the altar. Whether it was the Goddess or the Christian God, we may never know. If the spirits deem me high priestess, the Druids will be in harmony with everyone. If there are entities that wish to harm Beith, we will banish it! Beith shall suffer no more if I am high priestess. We will not have anyone like Agnes in our grove again."

"You say that with conviction," McGowen said.

"I trust her, and I believe her," Brandon said. The camera then panned to Brandon.

"Please, tell us why, if you are comfortable doing so," McGowen said.

"I lost my younger sister. Anna's mother knew that, and she knew about the altar. She could have stopped it at any time but didn't. Who does that? She allowed her daughter to die in the process to save herself. What mother does that?" Brandon raised his voice as though he wanted to yell.

The camera then moved back to Jessica McGowen.

"As you can see, Dave, there is both celebration and misery that is tied to this newfound freedom," McGowen stated to the news station.

"Our thoughts and prayers go out to the people of Beith for sure. Do we know when the Druid ceremony is tomorrow? And do you know if people are allowed to witness this ceremony?" Dave asked.

"Let me get confirmation from one of the Druids," McGowen stated. She then continued. "Dave, it will be at high noon tomorrow at the west side of Kilbirnie Loch. I was told that they do not mind visitors, but they ask that they respect the ceremony as it requires complete silence. That means no cameras or filming of any kind during the ceremony, Dave," McGowen stated.

"Well, we hope the ceremony goes well tomorrow, and thank you for covering this story, Jessica. It has definitely been a long road for Beith, and we are happy that they can start healing and hopefully getting back to their lives without fear," Dave said with compassion.

"Thank you. Indeed, it has been a long road. Just a quick fact sheet on this situation in Beith, Dave: the shadow has been in control of Beith for fifty years; Agnes Aird was the keeper of the altar just for the mere fact of keeping whatever higher power she received from her aunt after she died. What is unique about that is her aunt was the second minister of Scotland up until the time of her murder. And there have been over seventy deaths here in Beith since all this started back in 2030. That's almost two deaths per year. Such a tragedy. Back to you, Dave," McGowen said.

The camera faded back to the newsroom, and Dave and his co-anchor continued with the news of rising power prices looming for the new year.

Beith was exceptionally warm for this time of year. A beautiful, sunny sixteen degrees Celsius embraced the grove. It was delightful to see the last of the wildflowers still in bloom to enhance the celebration. Near the loch's waters was a firepit full of birchwood and a table draped with white linen where the chalice full of water stood. Old logs formed three rings around the pit for Druids to sit and to emphasize protection to the grove, and in between the logs were pink and white wildflowers.

Judy, the ovate, was today's master of the celebration, and she was preparing the area. The townspeople gathered above the grove along the road to witness the event. "Please be silent" signs marked the road every few meters. At high noon, the formal part of the celebration was to start.

"Isn't this exciting!" Judy exclaimed.

"Will the spirits allow a witch and Druid to be a high priestess?" Brandon asked.

"We must remember, Brandon, it is not up to our personal understanding. Our personal bias shades the true light and therefore diminishes our knowledge and wisdom. See the wolf, for example. There must be an alpha, but it is not made that way by the color of its fur or how loud its growl is. It is made alpha by its ability to lead the pack. Agnes was high priestess because of our own bias. Today, the spirits will choose, as it should be," Judy explained.

"You're right, Judy. I'm sorry. I guess I'm out of practice," Brandon said as he lowered his head in shame.

"We have all been without direction for a very long time. Rest assured, today, those days are gone," Judy said, giving Brandon a smile. She looked up and saw the rest of the grove walking toward them.

"It's time," Judy said.

Everyone was dressed in white robes with white ropes as belts. As they approached, they walked quietly toward the logs and stood until told to rest. On the north side of the circle stood Judy; on the west, Kristine; on the east, Jacquelyn; and on the south, Brandon. Latrice stood at the center next to the pit and was the only one wearing a nature wreath upon her head made with berries, twigs, and acorns.

"Brothers and sisters, please be seated," Judy said softly, and then she began with the ceremony.

"As we soon embrace the end of the harvest of Samhain and celebrate a new season, we also embrace the end of an evil era and celebrate a time of rebirth to the grove. Today, on the new moon, we will ask the spirits if Latrice will be chosen as the new high priestess."

"I, Jacquelyn, ovate of the grove, call upon the hawk spirit of the east. I ask for your wisdom and protection."

"I, Brandon, bard of the grove, call upon the wolf spirit of the south. I ask for your wisdom and protection."

"I, Kristine, ovate of the grove, call upon the salmon spirit of the west. I ask for your wisdom and protection."

"I, Judy, ovate of the grove, call upon the bear spirit of the north. I ask for your wisdom and protection. Spirits, we seek your decision and your decision only to determine if Latrice shall be the new high priestess. By flame is yes, and by ice is no."

As soon as Judy spoke the words, fire engulfed the pit. She just wanted to leap out of her skin but had to properly finish the ceremony.

"Rise, everyone! The spirits granted us their wisdom and blessing upon this grove. Please celebrate with me in introducing our true high priestess, High Priestess Latrice, Druid of the grove."

"Before we begin the celebration part, I want to thank the spirits for granting me this opportunity to prove that Druids can live in harmony with others. We only seek to give respect and peace to others, regardless of their faith, and to nature that surrounds us. My hope now is to rebuild the trust that was lost and build a better community here in Beith and throughout Scotland," Latrice boldly and proudly stated.

Everyone cheered, and the townspeople clapped and shouted, "Congratulations!" Brandon started playing his guitar. The grove started singing and dancing, thanking the spirits for their blessing. Jeremy and Christian, although not Druids, helped with providing food for the celebration.

Judy took the chalice and chucked the water onto the ground. She had started folding up the white cloth when Latrice approached her.

"Judy, stop. You of all people deserve to celebrate. You fought for what is right even when uncertainty blanketed the grove. If it weren't for you, dear friend, we might not be here. Thank you," Latrice said.

"High Priestess, that's very kind," Judy said with tears rolling down her face.

"Save that high priestess stuff for meetings. For now, let's go party, my ovate!" Latrice and Judy laughed and joined in the festivities.

After a month went by, the grove and town of Beith continued to experience peace and harmony, just as Latrice had promised. However, some pain had to be revisited before fully moving on. Latrice had the funeral for Catlin. It was nice to have everyone there. Even the councillor made an appearance in respect to Latrice. Then Daniel left for Edinburgh to live with his aunt and sister. Latrice sat on her porch swing, sipping her tea, reminiscing on the good times with friends and thinking about the good times to come.

On December 1, the first day of the last month before heading into year 2081, it was a sunny yet brisk two degrees Celsius. Agnes had been ordered to remain in her home without ever going outside unless some court ordered differently. With it being that cold, she had no issue sitting alone in her two-story home. Yet past the weather, the home sat empty. Thomas and Anna had both been taken as sacrifices. Daniel had left to be with Sabrina in Edinburgh. He couldn't stand the sight of his mother after what he learned about her. Daniel never saw Laurie again after the jubilee either. Agnes had to remain in her home. Not many neighbors had compassion for her, but the few forgiving lot offered to get her messages when she needed them. There would be times that she would see Nancy, John, and James go out as a family somewhere and wish she could go over to learn about the adventure Nancy had had that day. When Agnes would call her sister and ask to speak to Daniel and Sabrina, the only reply she received was to not call there anymore.

Random news crews from Glasgow and Kilmarnock would stand outside the house, hoping to get a glimpse of Agnes or some fresh news. She despised hearing the same mundane questions outside her door: "Do you regret what you have done? Do you miss your children? How is your health? How do you feel about people wishing you were dead?"

Agnes never really was able to state how she felt. Frankly, Agnes really didn't know herself. She had betrayed so many for so long that she had known what she did was wrong but believed there was no other way.

Looking out the window at the reporters in the cul-de-sac, readjusting mic cords and antennae, she assessed that it was time to address her thoughts. It didn't matter if Beith was ready to hear it, but she had to be heard. She finished her tea, rinsed out the mug, and slowly walked to the door. With slight indecision, she unlocked both dead bolt locks and opened the door. She stood knowing that at any moment, she could get shot at or killed by other means, maybe—but Agnes knew it was time. When the camera crews saw her, they snapped into action, running up to her door.

Without hesitation, one news reporter asked, "Mrs. Aird, do you feel guilty about keeping Beith under a shadow?"

"No questions, please. I will make the following statement, and then I will ask for you to not come back. I am quite certain with all I'm about to say, it will be enough for your papers, but more importantly, enough for Beith," Agnes stated. Then she took a deep breath and continued. "First and foremost, I wish to extend my deepest condolences to those that lost loved ones due to my misguidedness. There is nothing I can do to bring them back, and that I regret every day. Do I know that people want me dead? Every day I hear the vile death threats that come through the monitor. They have lessened some, but I cannot be upset with them since it was me that gave them their torment, their sadness. I miss my children very much, but the likelihood of me ever seeing them anytime soon is relatively naught. Although that hurts me to the core, and I understand, I hope that someday they will forgive me," Agnes said. She paused for a moment. News reporters didn't wait for information. They asked even when asked not to.

"How do you get your nourishment?" one news reporter asked.

"I have lovely, forgiving people who offer to deliver food for me. I don't eat as much anymore, but I stay busy cleaning and making quilts. I'm still healthy, and I currently do not have any issues," Agnes said quietly.

"Do you have anything new about how long you are in confinement?" the news reporter asked.

"No. The courts have not been confronted with this type of scenario before. Although I kept the altar hidden, I personally did not murder anyone. It could be a possibility that I could be held liable for manslaughter. I am really not sure as I haven't heard from my lawyer. He said he would call if there were anything new." Agnes shrugged her shoulders and looked blankly at the reporters. There was nothing more she really wanted to say. She did want to give the community an apology at the very least. They deserved that much.

"Is there anything else you would like to add, Mrs. Aird?" the news reporter asked.

"No. Thank you very much for your time," Agnes said. She turned around, not looking back, closed the door gently, and locked it. She knew there was nothing she could say that would change the hearts of Beith. Maybe one or two supporters at best, but nothing to get overjoyed about. The damage has been done.

By this time, it was 10:00 a.m. The reporters normally showed up around 7:30 a.m. in hopes of a glimpse. After today, she wouldn't have to worry about that anymore. Agnes had gone to get some material for her quilt when the monitor came on.

We are interrupting your regularly scheduled program to bring you this important announcement. The reporters wasted no time getting her statement blasted all over Scotland. Agnes looked at the screen and saw herself in the doorway. She thought to herself, she could have done something more with her hair. However, Agnes was certain no one truly cared. Just then, a call came through. It was Agnes's sister, Irene.

"Irene, I'm surprised to hear from ye," Agnes said in shock. She figured it was best if Irene controlled the conversation.

"I saw you on TV," Irene said.

"Ye," Agnes replied. She was clueless about what to say or whether she should respond. She didn't want to push for information about Sabrina and Daniel just yet.

"I can't say I agree with your confession, but I understand it," Irene said.

"What do you mean?" Agnes asked, confused.

"I mean, as you got older, you could have ended this and just sacrificed yourself. I know you've heard that plenty of times, but our family was different. Our grandparents got involved in dark forces that no one understood. Auntie Dawn got involved in it because she didn't want to disappoint Granny. Mum protected us and taught us the right way to respect nature and other people in their views. Yet somehow you got caught into the curse. It had to be from that visit when we all went to Glasgow to support Auntie Dawn in being the new second minister," Irene stated.

"I remember I was little, and she asked me to sign my name in blood to prove that I was a true Druid. Doing so would help me be a high priestess one day," Agnes said shamefully.

"Damn it! And I'm sure there is no way to find what you signed. That bitch passed the buck to a five-year-old!" Irene exclaimed.

There was a good minute of silence.

"Irene, are you still there, love?" Agnes asked.

"Yes, I'm here. Well, I did want to tell you that it is a joy having Sabrina and Daniel here. They still don't want to talk to you, but I wanted to let you know that they are doing well in school. Daniel is into rugby, and Sabrina is in track. Daniel helps his sister a lot, and both get along very well. You should be very proud of them, sister," Irene said lovingly.

"That's wonderful. Thank you so much for that. I really do appreciate it," Agnes said as she gave a sigh of relief.

"You're welcome. Take care. We will talk again soon," Irene said.

"OK, take care, sister," Agnes said.

They both hung up, and the monitor went back to the programme that had been on previously.

Agnes was relieved to hear about Sabrina and Daniel. Yet she missed Anna. Agnes took a deep breath and headed upstairs to Anna's room. She opened the door, and it was dark. So dark it felt like the essence of the shadow was there, as though to remind her of what she had done to Anna. To Beith. She opened the curtains, not allowing that darkness to set in again. Agnes opened the closet and saw all her clothes. She grinned a bit when she saw her wellies. Agnes touched her ruby earrings she was wearing, as the wellies reminded her of when Anna would go and search for gems. She shut the door and looked at the long tables Thomas had made for Anna to work on her jewel crafting. Anna had always been so lively and talented. Agnes smiled a little, then sat on her perfectly made bed. Then the floodgates opened. It was decades of hiding, decades of greed and power that poured down her cheeks. She was the person that she never wanted to be, yet she had even proved herself wrong. Whatever she had signed long ago had controlled her, her whole life.

Some time passed; it was noontime, and she figured it would be best to eat something. She wanted so badly to call Nancy and have her come over, but she knew that would never happen again. Agnes went downstairs and made some tea and little sandwiches when she received a message on the monitor. *They're coming for you.* It was from Nancy. Agnes didn't want to respond because she thought it was Nancy venting in her own way.

"Screw it," Agnes said feistily. She tried to ring back Nancy, but she didn't pick up. Agnes waited a few moments, and still nothing. She stood in the kitchen for a few moments but heard a commotion outside. She looked out the bay window in the living room and saw a massive crowd walking steadily, in unison, toward the cul-de-sac. They were all in dirty white robes, barefoot, and all had blank stares as though they were newly risen zombies. Some had bloodstains on their robes; some had blood only in their hair. People were running up to them and hugging them as though it was truly their loved ones back from the dead. Neighbors were yelling, *They're back! They're back!*

Agnes couldn't believe her eyes. Was she seeing Anna and Thomas in the front of the group? Was she seeing childhood friends for the first time in forty-five to fifty years? When people would come up to hug them, they didn't respond. It was like they were on a mission to get somewhere. People brought buckets of soap and water to try and clean them, but their steps were as if they were moving sluggishly yet together, like soldiers. The mass was unfazed, to say the least. Agnes went to open the front door to get a better view. Agnes could see Nancy standing on her porch with her arms folded and John holding her from the side. She looked at her neighbors to her left, and they didn't even bother looking at her but did yell out, "I hope they give you your sentencing, Agnes!"

By this time, the mass of the dead was standing at the edge of her driveway. She looked and recognised every single one of them.

"Agnes, is that you?" Thomas asked. He didn't look directly at her but in the direction of the house as though he had become blind.

"Yes, my love. Thomas. I'm right here," Agnes said happily. Thomas just stood there for moment and didn't move, even though he heard her.

"Mum, is that you for real?" Anna asked.

"My sweet Anna. I'm right here. Can't you see me?" Agnes asked.

"No, Mum. My eyes are not yet clear. I can hear you. Can I come home?" Anna asked.

"Of course, Anna. This is your home," Agnes said.

Thomas and Anna began to walk to house and through the front door.

"Do you remember this house?" Agnes asked.

Thomas looked around and said, "Yes."

"Do I still have my room upstairs? Can I see Sabrina and Daniel?" Anna asked.

Before Agnes could answer, the front door slammed shut, and the locks turned on their own.

"Aren't you happy to see us, dear?" Thomas asked. He then approached Agnes and gave her a hug, squeezing her tightly. There was no emotion to their hug. As he stared off into the distance, his eyes turned black.

The End

ABOUT THE AUTHOR

Kellyanne Hale is retired from the United States Army of 21 years, has a master's degree in terrorism studies, and currently works as a government contractor on Fort Huachuca, Arizona. Writing provides a way for Kellyanne to relieve stress, gather her thoughts, and discover her own creativity. When not writing, she plays and streams *World of Warcraft* under the name WOWSTARLORD; plays with her cats, Junior and Ollie; and makes home-made candles. Kellyanne has two lovely daughters, two grandsons, and lives with her two cats in Sierra Vista, Arizona.